SWORN TO PROTECT

RED STONE SECURITY SERIES

Katie Reus

Copyright © 2015 by Katie Reus

All rights reserved. Except as permitted under the U.S. Copyright Act of 1976, no part of this publication may be reproduced, distributed, or transmitted in any form or by any means, or stored in a database or retrieval system, without the prior written permission of the author. Thank you for buying an authorized version of this book and complying with copyright laws. You're supporting writers and encouraging creativity.

Cover art: Jaycee of Sweet 'N Spicy Designs
JRT Editing

Author website: http://www.katiereus.com

Publisher's Note: This is a work of fiction. Names, characters, places, and incidents are either the products of the author's imagination or used fictitiously, and any resemblance to actual persons, living or dead, or business establishments, organizations or locales is completely coincidental.

Sworn to Protect/Katie Reus. -- 1st ed.

ISBN-10: 1942447140
ISBN-13: 9781942447146

eISBN: 9781942447078

For Kari Walker. Thank you for all your insight since the beginning of this series and for being a true friend.

Praise for the novels of Katie Reus

"...an engrossing page-turner that I enjoyed in one sitting. Reus offers all the ingredients I love in a paranormal romance."
—Book Lovers, Inc.

"Has all the right ingredients: a hot couple, evil villains, and a killer action-filled plot.... [The] Moon Shifter series is what I call Grade-A entertainment!" —Joyfully Reviewed

"I could not put this book down.... Let me be clear that I am not saying that this was a good book *for* a paranormal genre; it was an excellent romance read, *period*." —All About Romance

"Reus strikes just the right balance of steamy sexual tension and nail-biting action....This romantic thriller reliably hits every note that fans of the genre will expect." —*Publishers Weekly*

"Prepare yourself for the start of a great new series! . . . I'm excited about reading more about this great group of characters."
—Fresh Fiction

"Wow! This powerful, passionate hero sizzles with sheer deliciousness. I loved every sexy twist of this fun & exhilarating tale. Katie Reus delivers!" —Carolyn Crane, RITA award winning author

Continued...

"You'll fall in love with Katie's heroes."
—*New York Times* bestselling author, Kaylea Cross

"A sexy, well-crafted paranormal romance that succeeds with smart characters and creative world building."—Kirkus Reviews

"*Mating Instinct*'s romance is taut and passionate . . . Katie Reus's newest installment in her Moon Shifter series will leave readers breathless!" —Stephanie Tyler, *New York Times* bestselling author

"Reus has definitely hit a home run with this series. . . . This book has mystery, suspense, and a heart-pounding romance that will leave you wanting more." —Nocturne Romance Reads

"Katie Reus pulls the reader into a story line of second chances, betrayal, and the truth about forgotten lives and hidden pasts."
—The Reading Café

"If you are looking for a really good, new military romance series, pick up *Targeted*! The new Deadly Ops series stands to be a passionate and action-riddled read."
—That's What I'm Talking About

"Sexy suspense at its finest." —Laura Wright, *New York Times* bestselling author of *Branded*

PROLOGUE

Quinn Brody scrubbed a hand over his face as he exited the empty squad room. He'd transferred to a new shift within the Miami PD less than a month ago and wasn't sure he'd fit with his new team. The guys were nice enough but something was off about their team leader. Nothing he could put his finger on, but Quinn had never ignored his gut.

Hoisting his duffel bag onto his shoulder, he headed down the quiet hallway toward the private exit. This part of the building was practically deserted this time of day. At least this way he wouldn't have to see any civilians or deal with any bullshit on his way out. He could head straight home, crack open a cold beer, watch whatever game was on, then crash. Heaven.

At a soft squeaking sound, he turned and saw Suzanne White, his team leader's wife, stepping around the corner. Her blonde hair was down in soft waves around her face. He'd only talked to her a handful of times and she was always so skittish. Maybe that was the reason he had a problem with his team leader. In his experience cops' wives didn't tend to be so damn jumpy all the time. He couldn't help but wonder what the reason behind that was. Especially since she was wearing sunglasses inside.

Quinn lifted a hand in greeting as he turned back around. "Hey, you looking for Glenn?"

She nodded and started to backtrack, taking two steps away from him. "Yes, but I'll find him." The words came out in a rush and he could hear the worry in her voice.

What the hell? He was a big enough guy, but Glenn was bigger, broader, so Quinn didn't think it was his size. Quinn's instinct propelled him forward, his gut telling him to talk to Suzanne. His legs ate up the distance of the hallway in seconds. "He's in one of the gyms, I'll walk with you."

She shook her head forcefully. "No, it's fine. I know where the gyms are." She took another step away from him. It was subtle, but hard to miss when her body language was screaming she didn't want to be near him.

When she shifted her purse against her side and winced ever so slightly, alarm bells went off in his head. Maybe he was overreacting, but...he was going to go with his instinct. "Your eyes bothering you?"

She glanced over her shoulder toward a set of elevators and a door that marked the emergency staircase. All the desks in the bullpen were empty since everyone was gone. It wasn't like that anywhere else in the rest of the building, but his team was on call the next four days and didn't have to be at the station so it was like a ghost town down here.

"I'm okay," she whispered, a tremble lacing her voice as she turned back to him. "I just...you don't need to come with me." The hint of desperation in her voice punched him right in the gut.

She was afraid. Of him? Maybe. But Quinn didn't think so. He let his bag drop and leaned against the nearest desk, shoving his hands in his pockets so he looked smaller or hopefully less threatening. "What's going on? Is someone... hurting you?" Because those damn glasses made no sense. Combined with everything else, yeah, something was off here. Unfortunately he had a sick feeling he knew exactly what it was.

She swallowed hard, then to his surprise let out a bitter laugh as she took another step back in the direction of the elevators. "Don't bother. I know how things work around here, how you all stick together. Do me a favor and don't talk to me again. Don't even look at me." Before he'd pushed up from his perch she was moving away from him at a fast clip, her sandals snapping against the tile floor.

He shoved up and beat her to the elevator, covering the nearest call button with his hand. "I'll do that if you really want. But I don't think you do... When I was about thirteen my aunt came to live with my family. She'd been in an abusive relationship and at the risk of blowing this out of proportion, so are you."

When she didn't answer, just stood there staring up at him with those sunglasses so all he could see was his own reflection, he continued. "If you need help, we'll head out one of the side doors and I'll take you somewhere safe." He was dead serious. The thought of any woman being beaten on made him feel sick.

She snorted and he was glad for the bit of attitude.

"I'm serious," he continued. "It's safe. I'm not even allowed past the gate because of my gender but I know the woman who runs the place. She can help you. We both will."

Her shoulders drooped and even though he couldn't see her eyes Quinn could imagine the hope draining out of them. "He'll find me," she whispered, dejection in every line of her slight frame.

"Not there he won't. I only know about it because I helped two women escape their abusers about a year ago and the owner approached me." After vetting him, Quinn later learned. His words were quiet but maybe Suzanne sensed the truth in his statement. Or saw it on his face. Whatever it was, he knew the instant she decided to take a chance.

She stepped closer to him now, pushing her sunglasses up on her head to reveal two black eyes. One was darker than the other, as if it was an older bruise. He contained his wince but he couldn't contain the surge of rage inside him. What. The. Hell.

"Normally he avoids my face but he's been getting more violent the past couple weeks. I… don't why. He thinks I'm cheating on him with pretty much any man that looks at me." She sighed, the sound so miserable and ragged it sliced at Quinn.

He remained silent, swallowing back his rage as he let her talk. He didn't want her to sense his anger and think it was directed at her.

"I just want to go to sleep at night and not worry that I'll wake up by being slapped or punched. I just..." Her voice cracked as tears streamed down her face. But she didn't break his gaze. "I just want to be free to live my life without fear."

Throat tight, Quinn nodded. He didn't touch her, just motioned that she could come with him. "You'll have to leave right now, with just the clothes on your back. We'll get your things later." He'd deal with that fucker Glenn later too. Quinn was going to report him no matter what. Just because Glenn wore a uniform didn't make him above the law. If anything, he had more of a duty to respect it.

"Okay." She nodded and placed a hand almost protectively against her flat belly.

It was a move Quinn had seen numerous times from pregnant women. In that moment a sense of new urgency spilled through him. He needed to get her to safety fast. They were silent as they hurried across the bullpen to the adjoining hallway. He wondered why Suzanne was accepting his help when he was virtually a stranger, but he figured the pregnancy, if she was indeed pregnant, had something to do with it. She'd have to be desperate now. Quinn planned to make sure her husband never hurt her again.

When they reached the exit door at the end of it, Suzanne placed a gentle hand on his forearm, the touch so light he barely felt her fingers skimming his skin. Her blackened eyes were full of shadows no woman should ever have to endure. "He'll kill you if he finds out you helped me."

Quinn held back the rage inside him, not wanting Suzanne to see it. She needed to feel safe right now. And if Glenn tried anything, Quinn would take pleasure in pummeling him. Let that bastard see what it was like. Beating on a woman half his size was weak, pathetic. Coming at Quinn wouldn't be so easy.

CHAPTER ONE

Six years later

"I'm telling you, the only guy I've dated since moving back to Miami freaked when he realized I was a virgin. From his reaction you'd have thought I said I wanted to set his dick on fire." Athena ran her finger up the stem of her wine glass, unable to hide a grin as her cousin Belle practically snorted out her champagne. It was hard to get Quinn out of her head, even two months later.

"Set his dick on fire, I like that." Belle shook her head and picked up her own glass as Grant, her husband of about a year, walked into the kitchen.

"Hope you're not talking about me," he murmured, moving straight for his wife like a heat-seeking missile.

If Athena didn't love her cousin so much she might be a little sickened by their constant displays of affection. Okay, not sickened, more like a teeny bit envious.

"You know I'd never hurt that part of you," Belle murmured, nuzzling Grant's chest.

"All right, enough of that while I'm in the room." Athena's voice was light as she took another sip of the bubbly cocktail. It felt good to hang with her cousin and relax. After two years of pretty much straight traveling for work, she was thrilled to be living back in Miami and surrounded by her huge, insane family. Especially Belle. She always felt like the two of them were the only somewhat-normal ones of the Manikas clan. Mostly. Belle was only a couple years older and they'd always clicked.

Grant just wrapped his arm around Belle's shoulders and leaned against her as he turned his focus on Athena. She and Belle had been sitting at the island in Belle's kitchen, chatting and drinking while waiting for everyone to arrive.

"So, whose man parts are you setting on fire?" he asked, quirking an eyebrow.

Almost two years ago, before he'd met and married Belle, Grant had been in an explosion that had left him scarred. Faded red marks covered the left side of his face and neck and from Belle, Athena knew he had more on his left arm and back. It certainly didn't take away from the raw power the man exuded. Plus he was a fighter—and would do anything for her cousin, something Athena adored about the man. For a moment she felt bad for joking about setting someone on fire but he didn't seem upset. Still, she needed to remember not to say anything like that in the future. "No one. I was just telling Belle about how I need to lose my virginity."

Aaaaand, that did it. He froze, his arm dropping from Belle's shoulders as he took a not very subtle step toward the entryway. "I need to get the door."

She picked up her tulip-shaped glass, fighting a grin. "I didn't hear the doorbell."

He ignored her and Belle's snickers, mumbling something under his breath as he hurried out.

"That was so freaking mean," Belle said through laughter.

"I know." Athena didn't bother to hide her own laughter now. "Your husband looks like a linebacker but the word virgin scares him? Seriously, what's wrong with men? I just want to get to the good stuff and have non self-induced orgasms. But I can't seem to get that first time out of the way." She had a vibrator, but an orgasm from a toy wasn't as satisfying as she knew it could be. In addition to seeing sex everywhere in the media, she had enough big-mouthed female cousins to know that. And while she wasn't looking for marriage she didn't want her first time to be with just anyone, someone she'd regret moments afterward. Maybe it was the way she'd been raised, but there it was.

Before Belle could respond, the doorbell actually did ring. There was an array of voices and when her new boss at Red Stone Security, Harrison Caldwell, stepped into the kitchen moments later with his beautiful wife on his arm, Athena slid her champagne glass to the side. She thought she'd been subtle but when he laughed she realized she hadn't been at all.

"You're not on the clock and I'm not here to work. But I am looking forward to your presentation on Monday." He shot her a quick grin before kissing Belle on the cheek and heading for the back door. Athena knew where he was going, too.

And if the expression on Mara's face was any indication, she knew what he was doing as well. "Men and their toys," she murmured, smiling at Athena as she followed her husband.

Grant, who was also Harrison's younger brother, had just gotten a new addition to his already ridiculously large grill that was apparently drool-worthy. Or something to that effect. Athena didn't really know or care. She was just as bad at cooking as Belle—much to her mother's continuing disappointment—and a grill was a scary thing.

"Is there anything you want me to do?" Athena asked Belle as she slid off her chair. They'd had the party catered—though Belle wasn't telling anyone but Athena that—so all the food and drinks were arranged artfully in the kitchen and on the lanai. And there was a full self-serve bar set up by the pool.

"Yes, enjoy yourself," she said as Lizzy and a slew of other people spilled into the kitchen.

As Belle started greeting guests, tall and gorgeous Lizzy, who also worked for Red Stone, hooked her arm through Athena's and dragged her toward the back door. "I know there's a bar out there and I'm kid free and done breastfeeding. I need a good drink."

"I'll make you something fun," she said, allowing herself to be propelled outside, laughing at her friend's enthusiasm. "Where's Porter?"

"With Grant, looking at a new gun." Lizzy shook her head as she spoke.

That was a little weird to Athena, but she knew the Caldwell brothers and pretty much anyone who worked for Red Stone Security owned more than one weapon. Most of the men and women in the security department anyway. They were all former military and it was like a thing with them. And they really liked to compare weapons.

She'd recently been hired as an event planner of sorts at Red Stone and her first official day was Monday—though she'd technically been working from home for the past three weeks to get ready for her first day. She was helping out with an event in Vegas in a little over a week and had needed to communicate with various companies out there. Coming into the office hadn't been necessary and she'd liked the freedom to make her own schedule these past weeks.

"Are you nervous about Monday?" Lizzy asked as they rounded the pool. It was filled with multicolored floating candles.

"A little bit. Not about the job, but the presentation itself I guess." For the last two years she'd done contract work as an event coordinator all over the world. Not local wedding type stuff, but big things—tradeshows and festivals. She taken her first job the week after she'd graduated college and because of her willingness to travel—and a lot of freaking hard work—she'd landed a lot of contract jobs. Some better than others. She'd majored in hospitality and minored in public relations, both of which had been an asset to her career.

In the beginning she'd had assistant positions but for the last year she'd taken on bigger projects solo. She shot Lizzy a look when she didn't say anything. Athena could read into the silence. "Okay, I'm nervous about the job too."

"You're going to do great," Lizzy said as they reached the mini Tiki bar. The air was cool in the high fifties and the scent of various meats on the grill filled the air. Even though they'd had the party catered, apparently Grant had insisted on grilling some things himself. "I wouldn't have recommended you apply for it otherwise."

Athena ducked behind the bar and grinned at the array of bottles and other garnishes. She'd been friends with Lizzy the past couple months and knew her friend's tastes by now. As she started mixing up their drinks she said, "If I fail, hopefully they won't blame you."

Lizzy just snorted but eyed the drink mix curiously. "Purple?"

"Just wait. You'll like it." She rolled the rims of the martini glasses in sugar as she spoke.

"Where'd you learn to do this?"

"I bartended a little in college and there were a few occasions on the job where I had to assist because staff called out sick for an event." There'd been a huge festival in Madrid she'd helped out with a year ago where three of the staff had gotten food poisoning, so in addition to everything else she'd been in charge of, she'd had to help with drinks on and off. That had been such a chaotic, ridiculous job.

"At least you'll have something to fall back on if you do fail," Lizzy teased.

"I seriously hope not." She set the two glasses on the bar and strained the purple concoction into them. With the twinkle lights strung up around the lanai and the ones glittering in the pool, the sugar seemed to sparkle around the rim. "This is called a wildcat."

"You have to make me one of those too!" The unfamiliar female voice made Athena look up.

Her eyes widened as her gaze locked with Quinn freaking Brody, the too-sexy-man with an aversion to virgins. He was with the tall woman who'd just asked Athena to make a drink. But she had eyes only for Quinn. Her heart about jumped out of her chest. What was he doing here of all places? At least he looked just as surprised to see her.

She ignored him because she knew if she stared into those dark eyes she'd lose the ability to speak and then she'd inevitably embarrass herself.

The tall, built-like-a-goddess woman with pale blonde hair he was with smiled widely at Athena. "Only if you don't mind," she continued, nodding at the drinks. "They look so good."

"Ah, you can have this one. I made an extra for the lush here." She tilted her head at Lizzy with a half-smile. Athena had planned to drink the second one herself but didn't trust her hands not to shake if she made another.

She couldn't believe Quinn was standing right in front of her, looking all casual and annoyingly sexy in dark jeans and a long-sleeved sweater shoved up to his elbows. Why did his forearms have to look so good?

"Ha, ha." Lizzy snagged her drink as Athena stepped out from behind the bar. "Athena, this is Quinn Brody and Dominique Castle. They both work for Red Stone but Dominique is almost as new as you."

Forcing a smile on her face, Athena nodded politely at both of them—and tried to ignore the way Quinn was staring at her. She'd had no freaking idea he worked for Red Stone. He looked a bit like a hungry wolf. Just like on their last date—two months ago. When he'd decided she was too much trouble, being a virgin and all. Jackass. "It's so nice to meet you both." She did a mental fist pump when her voice sounded normal. "I promised Belle I'd help out inside but I hope to see you both around tonight." *Liar, liar.*

"Me too. Thanks again for the drink," Dominique said cheerfully while Lizzy just gave Athena a strange look.

Athena wasn't sure what Quinn's expression was because she'd decided to do the mature thing—and studiously ignore him. When she looked at him it was just a reminder of all those intense kisses they'd shared. He'd lit her body on fire like no one ever had. They'd gone on half a dozen dates and she'd thought they were on the same page, had wanted the same thing. Obviously not, and she thought she'd been over it.

No, she *was* over him. She simply needed to get it together before she saw or talked to him again.

Lord, talk about totally unexpected.

Since she didn't know everyone at the party it was easy enough to make her way inside without having to make small talk. She hurried to Belle and Grant's bathroom, not bothering to use one of the guest ones. Not when she just wanted a couple minutes of privacy and she knew her cousin wouldn't mind.

As she shut the bathroom door behind her, she leaned against it and let out a stupid rush of breath she hadn't realized she'd been holding in. The man should not be able to affect her at all. Not two months after… the hottest dates of her life. She'd been so sure—

No. Just, no.

She would not think about those midnight dark eyes of his and the dirty things he'd whispered to her as he'd nibbled along her jaw, making his way to that sensitive spot on her neck.

When she suddenly wondered if he and Dominique had come here tonight together, as a couple, it was as if she'd been doused with that clichéd ice water. That certainly cooled Athena's thoughts down. Those two probably were together. Worse, they *looked* perfect together too. Both tall, sleek and too sexy for mere freaking mortals like herself.

Sure, Athena might be named for a goddess but she wasn't some siren. Ugh, and she'd worn a boat-neck cashmere sweater, jeans and ballet slipper type shoes.

Super sexy, she thought sarcastically, wishing she'd opted for heels at least. Even if she did think heels were ridiculous. At five feet two, she could use a bit of height but she liked her feet too much to constantly subject them to torture. God, just seeing him here, with someone so seemingly perfect for him, made Athena feel like that chubby girl in high school again. The girl with the big personality. The girl everyone wanted to be friends with. But not date.

She tried to shake off the old insecurities. Gritting her teeth at herself, she took a deep breath and opened the door. She wasn't going to hide in her cousin's bathroom and berate herself. She'd had a few dates with the man. It hadn't worked out. No big deal.

She was going to get another glass of champagne, enjoy herself and get to know her new co-workers. The thought came to an abrupt halt as she opened the bedroom door and found Quinn leaning against the wall opposite her, almost casually. But she wasn't fooled by his stance.

Nothing about him was casual. Those muscular arms were crossed over his broad chest and there was an almost predatory gleam in those dark eyes. No, that look on his face couldn't be mistaken for anything but raw lust.

Which wasn't exactly a shock. Their attraction to each other hadn't been the issue.

CHAPTER TWO

Seeing Athena again in person had been like a punch to all of Quinn's senses. Everything about her was sensual and he knew she wasn't trying. She screamed sex appeal and it was all in her big blue eyes and sultry mouth. Her bottom lip was perpetually pouty and drove him just a little crazy. He couldn't believe she was working for Red Stone or that she was at Grant's place. He knew she came from a huge family and seeing her again, now the resemblance to Belle was clear.

Her lips pulled into a thin line for a moment, her expression one of annoyance before it quickly morphed into what he thought of as her fake, forced smile. He'd seen it once when a waiter had been rude to them.

Quinn didn't like being on the receiving end of it. "It's good to see you again," he murmured, the urge to reach out and... hell, touch her, was so damn strong. And insane. He had no right to touch her.

Fake smile in place, she nodded once. "Yeah, nice to see you too." Then her brow furrowed as she looked down the hall then back at him. "What are you doing here?"

"Waiting for you."

"Oh." That smile faded only to be replaced by a look of bewilderment.

He wanted to reach out and smooth the lines of confusion from her forehead before claiming her mouth. He was a fucking idiot for walking away from her. The past two months he'd hadn't been on any dates. Though he'd asked two women out, he'd cancelled for both dates, claiming work as an excuse. After Athena everyone else was too bland, too... *not* Athena. He didn't want anyone other than her and that was disturbing.

She'd left her long, espresso-colored hair down in big waves he wanted to run his hands through. The last time he'd seen her she'd looked the same except for a single braid she'd fashioned as a headband of sorts. She'd told him it was Bohemian.

"Ah, I didn't say we'd met because I thought it might be weird," she continued.

He'd figured as much and he'd been too stunned at seeing her to say *anything*. He forced his gaze from her delicious mouth to her eyes. "When did you get hired by Red Stone?"

She lifted her shoulders in a jerky, awkward shrug and flicked a glance down the hall, as if she was biding her time to escape. "A little while ago. My first official day's not until Monday. Is Red Stone the same company you've been with the last six years?"

He'd told her that he was in private security but hadn't mentioned the name of the company and she'd been understanding. His rule was not to tell women who he worked for unless things turned serious. Things had never actually turned serious enough with anyone for him to be open about who he worked for. "Yeah. Listen, I'm sorry about the way things, uh, the way I..." Damn it, he'd never been tongue-tied around a woman before. Not even as a teenager. Looking at Athena now, he couldn't believe he'd been dumb enough to walk away from her. When he'd realized how innocent she was it had freaked him out, to put it mildly. Had made him feel guilty for the dirty things he'd said to her, wanted to do to her. With her—

Her annoyed voice cut through his thoughts. "I really don't want to talk about it. It's not a big deal." But her stiff stance and almost neutral expression said the opposite.

In his limited experience with her, her expressions had always been so open and animated. Now it was clear she was putting a wall between them. Even if he deserved it, it still irked him.

"Okay." He didn't really want to talk about it either. Clearing his throat, he continued, "Dominique is my cousin." For just a moment out by the bar there'd been a flash of something in Athena's gaze. Maybe he'd read into it, maybe not. Either way, he wanted it clear that he wasn't with anyone else. Not that he was sure it would matter to Athena one way or another.

For the briefest moment, relief flared in those Mediterranean blue eyes. God, those eyes. She wore a soft-looking pale blue sweater that made her eyes seem even brighter against the hue of her skin. Even though it was February it seemed she had a sun-kissed look all year. He wanted to run his hands over all her soft curves, pull her close and devour her mouth. Damn it, he needed to get his thoughts under control. He'd already fucked up with her before, he didn't need to sport a hard-on right now. That'd go over real well.

"She seems really nice," Athena murmured, taking a step into the hallway and away from him.

It took a second for it to register what she was saying as he was mentally ordering his dick to stay down. What. The. Hell. He'd always been in control of his body. Always. Being around Athena again reminded him of why he'd run. Well part of the reason. The virginity thing had been an excuse he'd used to convince himself to end things. Because he'd known that after her, he'd be turning in his bachelor card forever. There was something so sensual and raw about her that called to him on the most primal level he'd just known she could be *it* for him. Quinn hadn't thought he was ready for anything serious or to settle down.

Seeing her again, he couldn't believe he'd actually walked away. Over the past two months he'd tried to convince himself he'd built her up in his head. No such luck.

It was clear she wanted to head back to the party and he didn't want to make her uncomfortable so he tilted his head toward the end of the hallway. "Want to grab a drink?"

"That sounds good." A real smile touched her lips then, fleeting, but long enough for him to feel the effects of it through his entire body. "It was kind of a jolt to see you out there," she said softly as they headed down the hallway.

Something eased inside him at the slight shift in her tone. "Yeah, no kidding. You look like Belle, I can see the resemblance now." She was a little shorter than her cousin, but they were both knockouts.

She lifted her shoulders, no awkwardness there now. "Our fathers are brothers."

"On Monday I'd like to take you to lunch," he blurted. They'd reached the end of the hallway and he knew his time with her was limited. He didn't think she'd want to stand around talking with him much longer even if she did seem more relaxed. "Since it's your first day," he tacked on, even if it was a lie. He'd make it seem casual even if that was the last thing he felt.

A tactician by nature, he was going to play things right this time. Or give it his best shot.

"Ah…" She trailed off as they reached the end of the hallway.

It emptied into the oversized foyer where Grant, Belle and Carlito Duarte, a detective for the Miami PD, were talking.

Carlito—good-looking bastard—smiled at Athena with a familiarity that grated against Quinn's nerves. "Hey, Quinn. Athena, I didn't know you'd be here," he said, moving in to give Athena a hug like he had every right in the world to do so.

For all Quinn knew, the guy did. Athena didn't spare Quinn a glance as Carlito hustled her off toward the kitchen where the sounds of the loud partygoers filled the air.

"Who died?" Belle asked, drawing his attention to her.

Blinking, he looked at Belle and Grant to find her watching him curiously and Grant with an almost knowing expression on his face. "What... oh, I just need a drink."

There was a loud knock on the door, making Belle push out a laughing breath. "I'll get it," she said nudging Grant with her hip. "Go find a drink for Quinn and get me one too while you're at it."

Grant dropped a quick kiss on her mouth before clapping Quinn on the back. "I recognize that look," he said as they entered the half-full kitchen.

Quinn decided to play dumb as he made his way to an ice bucket filled with beers. He grabbed two, handed one to Grant. "What look is that?"

Grant just snorted as he took the beer then set it on the nearest counter. "She's my wife's cousin and a new employee. Tread carefully." There was an unexpected warning bite to his friend's statement as he pulled a half-empty champagne bottle from the same bucket and began to pour a glass, presumably for Belle.

Maybe the tone shouldn't be unexpected. Grant would consider Athena family. "I will."

"Good. Then we won't have a problem."

Quinn took a long swig of his beer, surveying his friends and co-workers talking, eating, laughing. It was good to see everyone having such a good time. Which was the whole point of this party. He'd heard that it had been Belle's idea even though she didn't work for Red Stone. She'd told Grant they needed to have another party to welcome some new employees and to let everyone get together away from work. Various people from work had barbeques often enough but this was different, more organized.

"Where's your dad?" Quinn was going to circle back to the topic of Athena—who must have gone outside with Carlito—but wanted to ease into it.

Grant snorted and leaned against the counter, picking his beer back up. "Watching his grandson—with his girlfriend."

Quinn joined him against the counter. "Keith's dating someone?" He'd known Grant's dad a lot longer than the last six years he'd been with Red Stone. He and Harrison went back all the way to their Marine Corps days and he'd met Keith during a leave.

Grant nodded, amusement on his scarred face. It was good to see him so happy and relaxed. "Lana Gonzalez."

"From the community center?" Keith would have about fifteen years on her but yeah, Quinn could see it.

"Yep. I think he's gonna propose."

That was definitely a surprise but it made Quinn smile. "She's good people."

"Hell yeah." Then Grant lifted his shoulders. "Besides, she makes him happy and he deserves it."

"Anyone who puts up with you and your brothers definitely deserves it."

Grant just laughed in agreement before taking a sip of his beer.

Screw it, Quinn needed to know what he was up against. "So, Athena and Carlito? They together?"

Grant glanced at him, beer halfway to his mouth, which split into a huge grin. "I was wondering how long it would take you to come back to that."

Quinn gritted his teeth. "So?"

"I should make you sweat it, but they're not together. I heard her tell Belle he's too pretty and too much of a player."

A bark of laughter escaped. "That sounds like something she'd say," he muttered. As soon as the words were out, he inwardly cringed.

Grant's eyes narrowed a fraction as he took another pull from his beer. "How would you know?"

Crap. "We went on a few dates a couple months back." Six dates to be exact and he'd been like a man possessed. Right about now, thinking of her outside talking and flirting with Carlito, he wanted to kick his own ass. Being tied to someone like Athena wasn't a bad thing. But some fears ran deep, especially after his only real relationship died a fiery, bitter death.

Now Grant's expression morphed to one of amusement and something else Quinn couldn't define. Shaking his head, a ghost of a smile flickering across Grant's mouth, he picked up the champagne glass and moved away from the counter. "Watch your junk, man."

Frowning, Quinn started to ask him what he meant but the back door opened and the sound of Athena's laughter filled the air, rolling over him and wrapping around him. Out of the corner of his eye he saw Grant headed toward Belle but all Quinn's focus was on Athena. Who was unfortunately still talking with Carlito.

That was okay. Quinn would bide his time. If he could get her to agree to go out with him again, he wouldn't make the same mistake twice. No way in hell.

* * *

Glenn White stared at the most recent email message then closed the program on his phone before tossing it onto his kitchen counter. Another fucking rejection letter. This one generic. At least the company had responded at all. Some never did.

Finding work was hard enough but with his prison record it was proving impossible. Any type of law enforcement or security was out because of the crime he'd been charged with. That thought brought up a wave of rage.

He was lucky he'd had family to watch his finances while he was in prison but his money wouldn't last forever. He needed a damn job.

And not something menial. Before he'd been put away he'd been respected. Now, most of his former friends wouldn't talk to him.

They just didn't understand. Almost no one did. If his slut of a wife hadn't pushed him, hadn't talked or looked at other men so often he wouldn't have had to punish her, keep her in line. It was her fault. She'd sometimes gone out of her way to provoke him. He knew it with utter certainty.

If it wasn't for her and Quinn Brody he'd never be in this situation.

Glenn's hands balled into fists as he jerked open the refrigerator door. A beer would take off the edge and after six long years of shitty prison food, he was going to eat and drink whatever the hell he wanted. The only good thing about being locked up was that he'd had a lot of time to work out. He was in better shape now than he'd ever been.

His wife—ex-wife if you wanted to get technical—would never cheat on him again. He'd make sure of it. If he could just find her. It was like she'd fallen off the face of the earth. He'd find her eventually though. He'd never stop searching. At least Quinn wasn't hiding.

That bastard was just living his life, not a care in the world despite what he'd done. Not for long though. Glenn was going to make Quinn suffer first.

It was Quinn's fault his wife had left him, pressed charges against him. She'd made him out to be a monster. Glenn knew deep down that she must have been sleeping with Quinn. That bastard had manipulated Suzanne, preyed on her weakness. That had to be the reason she'd turned on Glenn and their marriage vows. It was the only thing that made sense.

Sure he'd had to punish her sometimes but they'd had so many good times. The sex had been amazing. He knew she hadn't been faking with him, not in the bedroom. If he could just find her, remind her how good they'd been together. He could convince her to come back to him. Make things like the way they were before. He just needed to see her, talk to her. He'd never stopped loving her. And no one would ever love her as much as he did.

His fist clenched around the cold bottle and he realized he'd drank all of it. Blinking, he looked around the empty, sterile kitchen. This place was a hole, but it served its purpose. He just needed a place to rent, to sleep at night. His parole officer could stop by at any time but he wasn't worried about her.

Glenn wasn't worried about anyone but Quinn.

Decision made, he knew that the time had come. He needed to take care of Quinn before he could move on. He'd gotten out of prison a month ago and couldn't find a job, couldn't focus on anything. It was impossible to move on knowing that bastard was out there enjoying his life. He'd have to be careful about it though because no way in hell was he going back to prison.

And Quinn must know where Suzanne was.

She was too stupid to disappear without help. When Glenn started to think about her living without him for six long years, that red haze descended, making it hard to breathe. He chugged his next beer, enjoying the coolness as it went down. Suzanne hadn't respected their marriage vows when they'd been together so he was certain she hadn't respected them since he'd been gone.

It didn't matter that they were divorced—that she'd divorced him. She belonged to him. Always would.

He grabbed another beer and headed to his bedroom. He opened the bi-fold closet door and arousal swept through him at the sight of Suzanne. On the interior wall of the closet he'd put up a picture of her on their wedding day, looking off into the distance, surrounded by white flowers. She looked so perfect and they'd been so happy then.

Until she'd begun disobeying him, flirting with other men.

His head started to hurt as he tried to figure out where things had gone wrong; when she'd started to change, to provoke him. His gaze shifted to the right of her picture where another picture was positioned.

Of Quinn.

Seeing it reminded Glenn of what had to be done, who had to be destroyed. He refused to go back to prison but he didn't mind getting his hands dirty with Quinn. Not one bit.

CHAPTER THREE

A buzz of energy hummed through Athena as she stepped out of the elevator onto her floor at Red Stone Security. She hadn't expected the majority owner, Keith Caldwell, to be at her presentation this morning. People always said he was so intimidating but the truth was, he reminded her of one of her uncles so his presence hadn't fazed her. It was Harrison Caldwell, his son, who had a sort of edge. Nothing she could really put her finger on but the guy was a teeny bit scary. Or maybe intense was the right word.

Either way, the presentation had gone well. Some of the security stuff for her first event would need to be ironed out because that certainly wasn't her strong suit. Everything else though; it felt like she'd just fallen into the right position here. And being able to stay in one place—for the most part because she would still travel about fifteen percent of the time—was heaven.

As she neared the end of the short hallway she heard a familiar male voice, followed by the laugh of her assistant. Freaking Quinn. Of course he'd have to stop by on her first day. She'd chatted with him once more on Friday night but had gone out of her way to avoid the sexy man without seeming like she was. It had been easy enough considering how many people had been at the party.

At least she felt better prepared to see him today. She'd worn black pants with a skinny belt and a pale blue silk top under a tailored jacket that narrowed at her waist, making her look slimmer than she was. Even though she hated them, she'd worn four-inch heels. She'd kept her jewelry a little boring and business casual, at least for the first day. Athena had seen Lizzy this morning before her meeting and her friend had said Athena looked fierce. Right about now, she felt fierce. Perfect timing to be confronted with Mr. Sexy.

When Athena stepped out into the open assistant's area, her heart skipped a beat to see Quinn standing next to Raegan's desk.

And he was wearing a *suit*. She might have to check for drool in a second.

She'd never gone for corporate types before and the thing was, Quinn didn't *look* corporate. He looked like he'd be more comfortable wearing military fatigues and carrying around one of those big guns she didn't know the name for. He was wearing a suit because he had to. Which made him even sexier. There was no way to hide all those sleek predatory lines and muscles.

Sweet Lord the man looked divine. Best. Suit Porn. Ever.

That was when she realized Raegan and Quinn had stopped talking. Crap, how long had she been staring?

Not too long if Raegan's casual expression was any indication.

"How did it go?" Raegan asked, her bright smile so big and welcoming it was hard not to adore the woman even though they'd only known each other a week. They'd spent time together before Athena's first day so today would go smoother. The fact that Raegan was Keith Caldwell's niece was a little weird but Athena had learned enough about their family dynamics that she knew Raegan wouldn't keep this job if she wasn't good at it.

"Ah, good I think. Really good."

"Was Uncle… uh, was Mr. Caldwell senior excited about it?"

Athena bit back a grin and nodded. Raegan was pretty much fresh off the farm—literally—and had moved to Miami only six months before from a tiny Midwest town and was trying so hard not to play on her relationship with the Caldwell's. But Athena didn't mind. "He was. Harrison was harder to read until the end and they've got some security concerns but I think it went well. How do you feel about going to the Vegas tradeshow with me next week?"

Raegan's eyes widened but the woman just nodded and seemed to struggle with not getting too excited. "That would be great. Thank you."

Smiling, she glanced at Quinn. "Hey, is everything okay?"

"Yeah, just wanted to see if you wanted to grab lunch." His expression was once again intense and even though those dark eyes didn't leave her face she felt as if he was undressing her with his eyes. She hated that he'd seen her partially naked. Sort of. They'd gotten so far as him taking her top off. Not her bra though.

Worse, she wanted to get naked with the man. Full-on, skin-to-skin. Gah. Stupid attraction. Athena cleared her throat, thankful she didn't actually have to lie. "I have an appointment but—"

"It was rescheduled when you were in with Harrison and the others," Raegan said oh-so-helpfully. "I moved some stuff around and sent the revised schedule to your email and synced all your accounts."

Though Athena was annoyed, Raegan was just doing her job, so she didn't show it. "Thanks." She looked at Quinn, keeping her expression as neutral as possible. "I'll meet you in the lobby in half an hour?"

He paused, his gaze sweeping to her mouth for just a moment before he nodded. "Looking forward to it," he murmured. Then he was gone.

How he managed to make that simple statement sound almost sexual was beyond her. Once he was gone and out in the hallway, she waited a moment, then peeked around the corner of the wall to see him disappearing into the elevators. His ass looked amazing in the suit too. Figured.

"Are you two together?" Raegan asked innocently as Athena turned back around.

"No. Just friends."

Raegan nodded once but it was clear she didn't believe Athena. "Oh, okay. I just met him for the first time today but he seems interested in you. A lot."

Athena didn't want to talk about her personal life at work. At least not on her first day and not until she knew Raegan better so she gave a non-committal shrug. "I'm going to check the schedule for the changes you sent me but after lunch do I have any free time?"

Raegan nodded. "About forty-five minutes before your first conference call."

"Good. Plan to meet with me in my office then. I want to go over some of the Vegas details and we can do some brainstorming."

Raegan blinked once in surprise but said, "That's great."

Athena hurried to her office and did a quick scan of her schedule for the rest of the day and the full week. It was jam-packed and for that she was grateful. She didn't like having spare time at work. Staying busy made her happy and feel useful. She knew she'd have to prove herself here, especially in the beginning, so she wanted to tackle everything full force. It was too soon to know for sure, but from what Athena had read from Raegan's resume and the woman's general attitude, Athena had a feeling she would be a big asset.

After she'd caught up on what she needed, Athena shelved thoughts of work and picked up her purse, coat and stood. She hoped they'd be walking somewhere since she wasn't taking a long lunch or even her full hour. Definitely not on her first day. There was simply too much to do.

Downstairs she found Quinn in the spacious, quiet lobby talking to a man with a Mohawk. The hairstyle seemed out of place but the guy was tall and ripped just like Quinn and had that same military air about him.

Quinn straightened slightly when he saw her, his look going all predator again and sending her mind into a tailspin. What was up with him? She didn't do hot and cold so during this little lunch she was going to make sure he understood they were just going to be friends. Not that she particularly wanted to be friends with him, even though she did genuinely like him. But she could do the mature thing since they were working together.

He was the one with the issue anyway and he'd had his chance with her. Since he'd lost it, anything else happening between them past friendship was a moot point.

She smiled at both men as she approached, shoving all those pesky thoughts aside. Time to put her game face on.

"Athena, this is Travis Sanchez," Quinn said, making quick introductions.

The big man nodded once, an easy smile on his face. "I've heard good things about you from Noel."

Athena blinked once before recognition slid into place. "You're Noel's husband?"

He nodded once, that smile still in place.

"Man she can make some serious hot chocolate." Athena had been at Lizzy's place when Noel had brought her own baby over for a 'play date' with Lizzy's boy. Since neither kid could walk or talk it wasn't much of a play date as far as Athena could tell. It had been more like a reason for the women to talk and relax—and she couldn't blame them.

His face flushed with pride. "Yeah, she makes everything from scratch. I was just telling Quinn that you two should head over to her coffee shop. They do Paninis, salads, soup and stuff like that. You can walk there and the service is fast."

She looked at Quinn, eyebrows raised. "Sounds good to me."

He nodded once.

After saying goodbye to Travis, who was heading back into work, she walked out with Quinn. A cool rush of air rolled over her as they stepped out into the bright day. It might be in the fifties, but she didn't bother with her coat. Not when there were no clouds in the sky and the sun felt so good against her face. "I can't wait until it's spring," she murmured, putting her sunglasses on.

"Summer's my favorite," Quinn said, doing the same with a pair of aviator-style shades that made him look too sexy for his own good.

The street was relatively quiet, with a few people strolling down the sidewalk all bundled up since Florida was actually having a winter. It wouldn't last though, she knew. She'd grown up here and in a couple weeks all those coats and scarves would be in storage for another nine or ten months.

She let out a light laugh at his comment and shot him a quick glance. "I'm guessing because it's bikini weather."

He snorted. "It's been a long time since I've worn one."

She nudged him with her elbow. "Ha, ha. You know what I mean."

He just lifted his shoulders in a casual gesture that shouldn't have affected her at all. But just being near him had her adrenaline pumping. Another good reason not to bother with her coat. It was as if being in his presence just heated her up from the inside out.

"So your meeting was good?" he asked as they reached the cute shop with outdoor seating. He held open the door for her and she couldn't help but notice the way he scanned their surroundings, as if it was second nature.

Athena had noticed that Grant and pretty much anyone who worked for Red Stone Security did the same thing. They were always on alert for any sort of danger. After traveling across the globe, she could appreciate that. "Yeah, I think so. Harrison's hard to read but I have a feeling he'd tell me straight out if he was unhappy with anything. Of course it's too early for him to be unhappy with me."

"Forgive my ignorance," he said as they got in the short line. "But what exactly is your position? I'm a little unclear on the details."

"Well, they've basically created a new position. Not for me specifically, but I'm a good fit." Or she really hoped she would be. "You obviously know how many different functions they provide security for?"

When he nodded she continued. "They're always expanding and now instead of just providing security, they're being asked to host or set up events taking place in Miami. I'm basically going to be an event coordinator for all local events—and an upcoming tradeshow in Vegas, but that's a little different." Something she didn't plan to get into now. "They want me—along with a team—to make sure the event isn't…"

"Boring, military, staid?" he asked, making her laugh as they reached the counter.

Smiling, she nodded because he was dead on. "Pretty much."

After they ordered, he paid for her food—much to her annoyance—telling her it was because it was her first day, but she wasn't so sure. It wasn't worth making an issue over, however.

Travis had been right because the service was quick. With her iced green tea and salad, she and Quinn managed to snag the last table outside. Considering the gorgeous weather it seemed everyone else had the same idea as they did.

Once they'd settled at their table, Quinn threw her for a loop when he asked, "So what's up with you and Carlito?"

Thankful she had her sunglasses back on to shield her eyes, she paused with her drink halfway to her mouth. "What do you mean?"

"Are you two dating?" Even though she was glad for her own sunglasses, she hated that Quinn had his on too.

All she could see was herself in the reflection. She shrugged, deciding not to give him a straight answer. It really wasn't any of his business. "Why do you care?"

"I want to know what kind of competition I'm up against." He took a bite of his Panini, his body language casual, as if he hadn't just shocked the hell out of her.

Okay then. If he was going to be blunt then she was too. "You ended things with me, Quinn."

His jaw tightened. She was glad for the little sign that he wasn't as calm as he wanted to put off. "I was a jackass."

"No arguments here." She let out a quick laugh and took a bite of her lunch.

"I'd like to take you out again. On a real date."

Well, hell. Of all people she appreciated honesty. She didn't like playing guessing games with people and in her job so many often couldn't be straight with her about what they wanted. Or they were simply indecisive. A serious pet peeve of hers.

"Nothing about me has changed, Quinn." Which, yeah, she could have tried to play coy about *that,* but screw him. She wasn't going to pretend to be something she wasn't. It had taken her years to get over her insecurities and okay, she actually hadn't gotten over them.

Not completely. She needed to know where she stood with people. It made her feel grounded, she supposed, in control. And he'd just completely pulled the rug out from under her when she'd trusted him enough to be open with him. "Still a virgin."

He shifted in his chair and she couldn't tell if it was from embarrassment or something else. "I wasn't sure, but yeah, I figured."

"So what, it doesn't bother you now? Or you just got jealous when you saw me with Carlito and decided to act all caveman?" Now that he'd thrown down with the honesty, she was going for broke. She wanted to know what had changed for him in the last two months and the truth was, she felt like she deserved the truth. He'd hurt her more than she wanted to admit.

Sitting back in his chair, he rubbed a hand against the back of his neck. "Shit, not pulling your punches, huh?"

She shrugged.

"I haven't been able to get you out of my head the last two months. I screwed up, and seeing you made me realize how much." He leaned in closer now. "I... I've never been as attracted to someone as I am to you." His voice dropped an octave as he said the last part, the deep quality of it sending a shiver racing through her.

She refused to let him affect her. They had a serious physical attraction, something she had no problem admitting. She couldn't deny it anyway because it was like an electric thing, almost tangible. But he'd freaked out on her once, she wasn't going to deal with that again.

"Look, I..." She struggled for the right words, not wanting to be too harsh. "Our attraction is intense, no denying it. But I'm not interested in pursuing anything with you other than friendship." And she wasn't going to give him a reason why either. She didn't have to and didn't feel like articulating why. He'd lost his chance, simple as that.

With his shades it was impossible to read his expression so when he nodded once and said, "Okay," she was a little taken off guard.

Maybe she'd expected more of an argument. She should be happy he was agreeing with her, not second guessing herself. But she wasn't going to sit here dwelling on it. Instead she asked him about his current job and how it was that he had a free lunch today. She knew most of the security people weren't in the office with much frequency, not with their erratic schedules.

As they fell into an easy rhythm of conversation she found herself oddly disappointed when their lunch break was over and they headed back to the office. If only she wasn't so attracted to him, maintaining a friends-only relationship would be a breeze.

* * *

Athena shivered as she reached for another eggplant to put in her basket. The local grocery store was colder than outside. After today she was exhausted and ready to kick her feet up at home with a glass of wine. She might not cook well but there were a few staple meals her mom had taught her how to make—that Athena had actually bothered to learn—and eggplant parmesan was one of them. It was so stinking easy to make, too, and she really didn't feel like takeout. After years of living on the road, there was something to be said about cooking at home.

Tingles danced across the back of her neck, making her straighten. She glanced over her shoulder to see a blond-haired man staring hard at a bag of apples. As if he couldn't decide whether to buy them or not. She'd noticed him earlier when she'd been in the aisle with all the pasta and sauce options. And before that when she'd been looking at various cheeses.

The store was big enough that it wasn't odd they were in the same sections, but she could almost swear he'd been staring at her a couple times. As if he knew her or something.

It was unsettling.

That was when she realized he didn't have a cart or handbasket. Turning halfway to the side, she ignored him as she looked at cauliflower heads, but now she knew what had been bugging her all along. He'd just been going up and down the aisles without picking up anything.

Out of the corner of her eye she watched him put the apples back and look at her again. She wasn't imagining it this time either; he was tracking her. Maybe that was too strong of a description but she didn't care. She'd traveled enough to know when to pay attention to people.

Taking a steadying breath, she decided to go straight to the manager. The owner was friends with her parents so she'd just ask someone to walk her to her car after purchasing her items. Even if she hadn't known the owner she'd ask for help anyway. She'd read enough horrible stories to know what could happen to women alone in a parking lot—before or after dark. There was no way she was ignoring her instinct with this.

Ordering herself to remain calm, she moved to another section of fruit and picked up a small mesh bag of mandarins, her favorite snack food. When she glanced back over, the man was gone. Feeling a little silly, but not enough to disregard her feelings, she put the bag in her basket and headed for the front of the store. She'd seen a few employees idly talking by a cash register earlier because there didn't seem to be too many people here right now.

As she rounded the corner of the produce section she almost ran right into the tall, blond man. Her heart jumped in her throat but she reminded herself she was in a public place. All she had to do was scream if he did something.

Using her basket as a shield in front of her, she kept her gaze on his and took a step to the side. He moved with her, his look menacing.

"Move out of my way," she demanded. Loudly. Her mother had taught her and her three younger sisters that with people who could be potential threats, the only way to respond to them was with force—because it was usually the last thing they expected.

He blinked, as if she'd truly surprised him.

Well, good.

Then he regained his composure and a smile lit up his face. "Sorry, honey, didn't mean to get in your way."

"Yes you did." She took a small step back, needing to put some distance between them. She might be able to scream but that didn't mean she wanted this guy to hurt her before she drew attention. And something in his dark eyes said he'd take great joy in doing just that.

There was something wrong with him, a wild gleam in his eyes that made all the hair on her arms stand at attention. Physically, he was a really good looking man. Kind of like a Ken doll but with scary eyes. And a tattoo peeking out from beneath his sweater. Not that tattoos were bad—Quinn had a few himself—but she saw a snake head with red eyes that looked well, creepy. Just like the man in front of her.

She'd taken him off guard again, she saw, when he blinked in that same surprised manner. Then his jaw tightened a fraction, his gaze narrowing before he glanced around. Athena saw exactly what he did.

An elderly couple standing by the end of an aisle discussing whether to buy a higher priced box of organic pasta or their normal choice, and two teenage clerks flirting with each other instead of working. Not much of a protection, but it seemed to be enough of a barrier to make him take a step away from her.

But not completely and he didn't move enough out of her way so she could bypass him. He was definitely trying to use his size to intimidate her, she had no doubt. Asshat.

He leaned down, but didn't actually step closer, his dark eyes seeming to glitter ominously. She knew that was her own imagination because for a long moment, she was rooted to the spot. Her throat tightened and in that moment she hated herself. Hated that she was pretty much frozen.

"Tell that fucker Quinn that his time is coming. No one close to him is safe," he growled out before snapping his jaws at her like a wild animal.

She jerked back, both from the action and the stench of beer coming off him in waves. Before she could think about responding, he turned and strode away from her. By the time he was walking out the sliding glass doors, she could finally move again, her breath rushing out of her in a huge whoosh of air.

The man's words were terrifying enough, but his eyes would give her nightmares. She knew it without a doubt. And how the hell did he know Quinn?

She also knew there was no way she was walking to her car alone or even with a manager. Setting her basket right at her feet, she pulled her cell phone from her purse with a trembling hand and called Quinn.

No matter what was going on between them—or rather wasn't going on—she knew he would be here as soon as he could. That was just the type of man he was. She had no doubt the owner would let Quinn see the video footage too. Let him see exactly who that man was.

CHAPTER FOUR

Quinn's heart was beating overtime as he pulled into the parking lot of the grocery store where Athena had told him she was. At this point all he knew was that a man had approached her, said something about Quinn's 'time coming' and basically terrified Athena.

He'd heard it in her trembling voice.

He was glad she'd called him though. That said a lot. More than he wanted to analyze right now. What she'd said at today's lunch had been a setback to his plans but none of that mattered.

The only thing that mattered was making sure she was okay and that she stayed that way. He did a scan of the parking lot, looking for any threats before pulling out his cell phone and doing an actual scan with his video capabilities. Just because he didn't see something didn't mean there wasn't a threat lurking nearby. Later he'd review the video and blow up images of license plates if necessary. But he figured this was probably useless.

As he got out of his truck, he automatically reached back to make sure his weapon was holstered securely at his back. He preferred a shoulder holster for work but this was better for now. He immediately spotted Athena's cobalt blue Volkswagen beetle and a small thread of relief spiraled through him at the sight. She'd assured him she wouldn't go outside and would stay in sight of people at all times. Then she'd texted him to tell him she was sitting in the deli.

Once inside the grocery store he immediately located the deli, which was clearly closed given that all the display cases had been wiped down and there was no food in any of the trays. But as he approached the entrance to the seating area, he saw her sitting at a small black table with two men on either side of her. Both looked concerned, the older man with dark hair and a thick mustache, patting her hand in a paternal gesture. The other had on a white button-down shirt and black pants. Over the shirt was a red vest with a nametag that read Steven. His expression was pinched, his stress lines around his mouth were deep. The two men were clearly related, probably father and son.

Athena saw Quinn before the men did and the second their eyes met he felt it like a gut punch. Her expression lit up with pure relief. She and the men stood at once.

The older man moved in front of the table in a surprisingly fast move, his body language clear.

"Stephanos, this is Quinn, my friend."

The older man just made a 'hmm' sound and stepped back, but his wary expression didn't change.

For just a moment, Quinn tuned the two men out since it was clear they weren't threats. "You're not hurt?"

he asked, sidestepping the younger man and moving around the table. Not caring what the strangers thought, Quinn rubbed his hands down her upper arms. She was wearing what she'd had on at work and her face was pale, but she looked otherwise okay.

"No, I'm fine. I keep thinking maybe I overreacted but my gut tells me I didn't." She shot a quick glance at the man named Stephanos, and whatever her look conveyed, the man just nodded once, then motioned to the manager.

"We'll be nearby if you need us." The man shot Quinn what could only be described as a don't-mess-with-her look before he and the manager strode away and out of earshot.

They only moved to the entrance of the deli where an unhooked chain 'separated' the small eating area and the rest of the grocery store. Looking back at Athena, Quinn took her hands and motioned for her to sit. He would have preferred to stand but she looked like she needed a break.

"Tell me what happened. From the beginning." He didn't drop her hands as they sat across from each other. He wished they were dating or in an actual relationship so he could comfort her more. Because right now he wanted to pull her into his arms.

She gave him a shaky nod. "Okay, and thank you for coming." He just grunted, not wanting her thanks, not for something like this, and she continued. "I just stopped in here to grab a few things. I didn't want takeout tonight and wanted to make something for myself that would last for a couple days of leftovers... And I'm rambling."

He just squeezed her hands. "It's okay. Take all the time you need."

Taking another breath that seemed to steady her, she started again. "I felt like this guy, this man, was following me or at least watching me. And not in the kind of way where he was working up the courage to talk to me, you know?"

He nodded, understanding perfectly.

"He was just sort of watching and following me around. I didn't realize that at first but when I was in the produce section it hit home that he didn't have a buggy or a handbasket. He wasn't shopping at all and he was doing a poor job of pretending. So I made the decision to go find Steven... Ah, Stephanos is the owner and Steven—whose name is actually Stephanos, too—is his son and the manager. It was just luck Stephanos senior was here. Anyway, I was going to go find Steven but the man, the stranger, sort of came out of nowhere." She shook her head, as if clearing her mind and when she shivered, Quinn wanted to punch the unknown fucker in his face.

He hated that anyone had scared Athena.

"I told him to move out of my way and I was intentionally, well, bitchy about it. I wanted to stun him a little."

That was damn smart. Quinn didn't respond though, not wanting her to lose her steam.

"He didn't move and for about a second he tried to make it seem like he hadn't intentionally tried to block my way, but his charm—and I use that word lightly—faded pretty fast. He told me, and this is a direct quote, 'Tell that fucker Quinn that his time is coming. No one close to him is safe'. Then... he sort of chomped at me, like a shark or wild animal. It was seriously creepy. And the guy had like, a violent energy. I know that sounds weird, but I was scared of him. And I'm pretty sure hurting people makes him happy."

Iciness chilled Quinn down to his core. He didn't have enemies, not truly. There was only one potential man who Quinn could imagine doing this. And the guy had gotten out of jail less than two months ago so it was a definite possibility. Stupid of the man, but a possibility. "What did he look like?" Quinn asked, all his focus on Athena, who was breathing steadier now and had more color in her cheeks.

She brushed at stray strands of hair that had escaped the low twisty thing she'd done with her hair. "Tall, like you, uh, white guy, blond hair and dark eyes. This might sound weird but he was good looking in that classic American way I guess some people might describe, but his eyes..." She shuddered and glanced down, swallowing hard before meeting Quinn's gaze again. "He looked wild-eyed, it's the only way to describe him. His eyes were dark and hollow. And I know he'd been drinking.

Or at least I smelled it on him. Oh, and he had a tattoo peeking out from his sweater sleeve. It was the head of a snake with red eyes."

Quinn frowned at the mention of the tattoo. Glenn hadn't had a tattoo back when he'd been in law enforcement, but things could have changed in prison. Quinn pulled out his cell phone and pulled up an old article about Glenn. It was a picture of him in his uniform—because the media had loved the idea of a bad cop, fucking vultures—next to the article about his trial. After zooming in on the face, Quinn handed his phone to her. "This him?"

Leaning closer as she took it, her eyes widened a fraction as she looked at the screen. "Oh my gosh, yeah, this is him. He's a little younger here, but yes, this is definitely him. Wait a minute, he's wearing... Is he a cop?" She whispered the last part, clearly horrified by the idea.

"Used to be. Not anymore. He just got out of prison a couple months ago."

Athena leaned back in her chair, her expression understanding. "You helped put him there, didn't you?"

Quinn nodded. He'd explain everything to her once they got out of here, but now wasn't the time for that story. He wanted her somewhere safer, where he could watch out for any potential threat. "Yeah. Listen, I'd feel a lot better if I could drive you home. I'll contact Grant and have him come get your car and—"

"Okay."

His eyes widened. "No arguments?"

She let out a shaky laugh. "Are you freaking kidding me? That guy scared the hell out of me. If you want to drive me home, I'm on board. What I don't get is, why would he have followed me here—and I'm assuming he must have. This obviously wasn't random."

Definitely not random. Which meant that fucker had been watching Quinn and had guessed that Athena meant something to him. Something he should have considered. But coming after Quinn was stupid. Beyond it in fact. It wasn't like he was the only one who'd had a hand in Glenn's arrest and prosecution. "He must have seen us at lunch today."

She shrugged. "So?"

"Honestly I don't know what his reasoning is. You're a beautiful woman and since he saw us together he might have thought you're important to me." Which she was.

"But... you said he got out of prison a couple months ago. Has he bothered any other women you've gone out with?"

Quinn snorted. "I haven't been out with anyone since you." Let her make of that what she wanted. Her lips parted in an adorably sexy way he'd seen her do a couple times when surprised but he didn't have time to dwell on that. Not now. "I need to talk to Stephanos about his security before we go and—"

"It's not working." She bit her bottom lip at his frown, but continued. "It's been on the fritz for about a week so they've got someone coming out Thursday to look at it. They've never had a problem here in the past since all the employees are either family or go to Steven and Stephanos' church so they didn't put a rush on it."

Quinn let out a growl of frustration.

"He's feels terrible," she whispered, leaning closer to him, moving so that their knees were touching. "And you're not going to make him feel worse."

A ghost of a grin tugged at his lips at her demanding tone. "Yes, ma'am," he murmured.

Her cheeks flushed pink. "Sorry, not trying to order you around."

"It's hot."

Now her cheeks went full-on crimson. But then she shook her head, as if dismissing his words. "Don't try to distract me."

He wasn't, but he didn't correct her, just stood. "Come on. I want to talk to the owner before we get out of here. Did you want to get your groceries?" She'd come here for a reason and he didn't want her leaving empty-handed.

"Steven already bagged them up for me. Said everything was on them, which is silly, but I think they just feel bad about the security situation. I tried to argue, but I know when I'm going to lose."

Quinn nodded his approval. He liked Stephanos and his son already. After talking to them and calling Grant to see if he could either pick up Athena's car or send someone else to get it, Quinn was getting Athena the hell out of here.

She might not realize it yet, but he was staying at her place tonight too. No way was he letting her out of his sight. She'd probably argue about that, but he'd face that when the time came. It was an argument Quinn wasn't losing.

Glenn White had regularly roughed up his wife, a woman he claimed to have loved. He wouldn't have a problem hurting a woman who meant nothing to him. And if Glenn thought it would hurt Quinn, yeah, he'd definitely come after Athena.

That thought was enough to send another frisson of raw fear punching through Quinn. Let White try. That fucker was going down if he came at Athena or anyone else in Quinn's life.

* * *

From the parking lot next door to the grocery store, Glenn remained hidden in the shadows as he watched Quinn exit with that smart-mouthed bitch. She was pretty, but that mouth of hers, the disrespectful way she'd talked to him... Glenn had wanted to backhand her just to wipe that look off her face.

Approaching her like that had been a test. Hell, he hadn't been sure if he would talk to her at all tonight, but when she'd gotten up in his face he'd wanted to scare her. He'd wanted to see terror in her eyes.

Now Glenn was glad he had because she clearly mattered to Quinn. He hadn't been certain if she meant anything to that bastard. She could have just been a co-worker. Today Glenn had seen them having lunch together, but that could have been a work thing. Sure, they seemed to have chemistry but there hadn't been any hand-holding or any other little signs they'd been a couple.

So Glenn had planned to tail her for a few days, to see where she went and who she visited. Following her would be a lot easier than keeping up with Quinn. Quinn was trained and would see a tail a lot quicker. Not the dark-haired woman whose name he was going to find out very soon. She'd been completely oblivious that he'd followed her from work. She'd stopped a couple places before hitting the grocery store.

Soon he'd find out her name and where she lived. He still had some contacts he could use, one in particular. Because following her tonight would be stupid, especially when it appeared Quinn was taking her home. Either to her place or Quinn's, it didn't matter to Glenn.

Now that he'd made contact, had let Quinn know he wasn't safe, it was time to play. Glenn hadn't done anything illegal and it was his word against some woman's if she said anything to the police. He was well within following the rules of his parole requirements.

He'd keep doing so for a while. At least until it suited him. He needed to buy a new ID and papers just in case he had to run later. He wasn't going back to prison but he wasn't stupid enough to think that he might not get caught going after Quinn. The new ID would be his backup. Though he still needed to lay his exact plans out, figure out his best plan of attack. That meant he'd have to watch this bitch, learn more about who she was, her habits, everything.

So if he had to flee, he'd be ready this time. No matter what happened, Quinn was going to get exactly what was coming to him and Glenn wasn't going back to prison. Never again.

CHAPTER FIVE

Athena caught Quinn's look of surprise as she gave him her address. He'd been about to plug it into his GPS until he clearly recognized the name of the street.

"You live next door to Belle and Grant?" he asked, glancing in the rearview mirror before reversing.

"Yeah, moved in a few weeks ago. She still hasn't let go of her old place and it makes more sense to rent it than letting it sit empty."

"I'm surprised they haven't rented it before now."

Athena shrugged. Since marrying Grant, Belle had been trying to decide if she should rent or sell and Athena moving back had given her an excuse to prolong making the decision to sell. "You don't want to talk about my living situation any more than I do."

Quinn let out a short laugh. "Not really. I need to make some calls, then we're talking. Okay?"

She nodded, letting him do what he needed to. Being with Quinn after that strange confrontation soothed most of the jagged edges of her nerves. Not completely, because that guy, Glenn White, had seriously scared her. Now that she knew he was a former cop the whole thing was even more worrisome. She was so thankful that Quinn was taking her home too because she didn't trust herself to drive. She was too shaky and for all she knew, the guy could have tried to follow her. At that sudden thought, she turned around in her seat.

Quinn, who was on the phone, she'd surmised with Grant, shook his head and held the phone away from his mouth. "I'll know if we have a tail," he murmured.

Okay then. She sat back against the comfortable leather seat and didn't wonder why he was taking all sorts of random turns. If someone was following them, Quinn would figure it out soon enough. It relieved a bit of pressure in her chest to know that he was trained.

She didn't live far from the grocery store, roughly about ten minutes, but Quinn had made enough turns that it took double that. By the time they pulled into the driveway, Quinn was getting off the phone with Grant—and Grant and Belle were waiting in the driveway.

Belle practically had the passenger side door open before they'd parked or Athena had unstrapped her seatbelt.

"Athena!" Her cousin dragged her into a surprisingly tight hug.

"You're squeezing really tight," she rasped out.

Belle immediately loosened her grip and stepped back, but not by much. She grasped onto Athena's shoulders and looked her up and down, as if looking for injury.

"What exactly did Grant tell you happened? I'm fine." Jeez, Belle had been through a heck of a lot worse over a year ago, being kidnapped by a crazed maniac who turned out to be a serial killer. Athena getting approached by a jerk in a grocery store wasn't on the same scale.

"I know, I just worry about you."

Athena just smiled, knowing it was their family way. Belle was only a few years older, but older cousins and sisters or brothers always looked out for the younger relatives. It was just the way it was, and something Athena was grateful for. "Thank you, seriously. But I swear I'm fine." She turned to look at Grant and Quinn, who both stood there like formidable warriors near the closed garage door.

"I've already swept the house," Grant started. Of course he would have. They had the security code and an extra key. "And I called in one of our guys to pick up your car. He said he'd call me if Stephanos gave him an issue, but I doubt he will. Stephanos and Steven were worried, so they'll be happy to help."

Athena simply nodded. They'd left her car keys with Stephanos and Quinn had said he'd contact the man when they'd figured out what they planned to do about her vehicle. "Is your guy bringing it here?"

Grant shook his head. "No, he's taking it to Red Stone where it will remain in secure parking overnight. I'm going to have it swept for bugs or trackers."

"Wait... what?" She stepped closer to Quinn and Grant, staring at her cousin-in-law as if he'd lost his mind. "This guy just approached me in a grocery store. Don't get me wrong, it was creepy, but sweeping my car for bugs, seriously? That's overkill." She figured that if he wanted to find her, he could just use her license plate number and attempt to track her that way. Thankfully she hadn't updated her address yet.

But of course the man just shrugged as if what he was doing was no big deal. Worse, Quinn didn't seem fazed by it either.

"I don't care if it's overkill," Grant said, his tone resolute. "I almost lost my wife to a serial killer. You're family and we look out for our own. Deal with it."

Athena blinked, realizing that even if she argued it would be pointless. There were certainly worse things than an overprotective family. "Okay, thank you."

Grant's eyes narrowed a fraction, as if he didn't quite believe Athena's acquiescence. Belle slipped her arm through Athena's, tugging her closer. "We're just worried about you."

Athena nudged Belle with her hip. "I know, it's why I'm not going to argue. As long as you don't tell my mom. Or your mom," she rushed on. If her mother or pretty much anyone in the family found out about this, they'd rush over to her house like madwomen with covered dishes and desserts. As if someone had died. She'd just started a new job and had a stressful day; she couldn't handle her family descending upon her.

"Well, *we* won't," Grant said before Belle could respond. "But you know Stephanos—"

"Oh, hell, I wasn't thinking," she groaned, wondering which of her family members would now show up tomorrow morning before she had to leave for work. Because she knew it was happening. There would be a little army of them. Her mom for sure. Not her sisters because they'd all be in school. But her mom, likely two of her aunts, and—

"Grant." Quinn's voice cut off her train of thought and internal pity party.

Athena looked between the two men as they seemed to have a telepathic conversation. Which she knew was ridiculous, but *something* passed between them as they stared at each other. Finally Grant nodded and they both turned back to her and Belle.

"I'm going to grab my bag from the truck and I think it wouldn't hurt to park in your garage. If you have the room." Quinn's first words since they'd gotten out of his truck could have knocked her over.

She knew she wasn't misunderstanding either. "You want to stay with me?"

"Either he stays over—in your guest room—or you stay with Belle and me... or I call your mother. If you let Quinn stay I'll call Stephanos right now and tell him to hold off on contacting your family." Grant gave her an easy smile that she wanted to knock right off his smug face.

"That's blackmail," Athena muttered. "And it worked." She shot Quinn a grim look. "You can stay." Definitely not the way she'd once imagined him staying at her place, but it was late, she was hungry and she wasn't going to waste any time arguing. "I'll go inside and open the garage door."

Quinn's expression was too hard to decipher. She couldn't tell if he was pleased to be staying with her. Though she wasn't going to admit it, and even if she did think this whole thing was overkill when she wasn't even a clear target, she was glad he'd be at her place tonight. She'd certainly sleep better with him under the same roof. She'd just have to ignore her growing attraction to him.

* * *

Quinn looked up from the island in Athena's kitchen as she stepped inside. He'd heard her on the stairs and knew she'd be here soon, but seeing her in the flesh still seemed to knock him back a few steps every single time. She'd already shown him to the guest room, where he'd left his duffel bag, and had told him she was changing out of her work clothes. While she'd been in her room he'd decided to put up her groceries and start on dinner for her.

Which clearly surprised her, given her raised eyebrows as she raked a gaze over him. "You're cooking?"

"Figured you could use the break." He'd already peeled the eggplants and was dipping the slices in egg yolk to roll in breading.

"I feel like I should tell you that you don't have to, but... I'm mentally exhausted and starving. So thank you." She gave him a tired smile and headed for her refrigerator. "I don't think I have beer or anything you'd like."

"Water's good for me." He motioned to the water bottle he'd grabbed earlier.

"You sure?"

He nodded, watching out of the corner of his eye as she moved to another counter and slid out a bottle of red wine before pulling down a glass from one of her cabinets. She was wearing a soft-looking gray and white striped sweater paired with gray lounge pants that fit snugly over her ass. He'd had a likely inappropriate amount of fantasies about what it would be like to run his hands over her ass—and entire body.

At that thought, his dick decided it had a mind of its own so he turned away and focused on the food. "How're you feeling?"

"Eh, okay. The whole thing is disturbing but you and Grant are right. I'd rather be smart about this while you figure out what to do—and I assume you're already doing something about White, right?" She pressed play on the small silver CD player on her counter and soft notes of jazz music filled the kitchen.

"Yeah. I've put in a call to an old buddy of mine from the local PD and he's going to find out who Glenn's parole officer is. What he did today wasn't illegal, and since no one else heard him, it's a case of he-said, she-said regardless. He won't be called in for questioning and there's nothing for you to do at this point other than just be aware, but I want someone official to know about this situation for the record." Quinn hated that they couldn't get Glenn on anything right now, but even drinking alcohol likely wasn't going to work against him unless Glenn's probation specifically stated he wasn't allowed to consume alcohol at all. And in Florida unless the crime was alcohol related, probationary terms usually outlined something along the lines of not drinking to excess. Which was too damn vague in Quinn's opinion.

"So," Athena said, taking a seat on the opposite side of the island across from him. "Who is this guy to you? Give me all the details."

He'd been ready for that question, and he owed her the truth. "Long story short, he was a wife-beater and I helped convince his wife to leave him." Quinn was thankful every day for how brave Suzanne had been. She'd been so terrified of her husband's position and looking back, Quinn realized what a leap of faith it had taken for her to come with him that day when he'd basically been a stranger to her.

"And he was a cop." Athena sounded disgusted, the words more of a statement than question.

"Yeah. He never should have been in the position he was, but he was smart. Suzanne, that was his wife, had been terrified to leave him. Things hadn't always been like that from what I eventually learned. Not that it would have mattered if it had been, but she married a different man than the one she ended up with." For the most part. The signs had been there, Suzanne just hadn't seen them. Most people wouldn't have because while Glenn was unstable, he was manipulative and smart.

For a moment, Quinn debated whether he should tell Athena everything, but decided for full honesty. There was no reason she shouldn't know, and to some extent she was involved with Glenn now too. "I was new to Glenn's squad, but during a chance run-in with Suzanne I realized she was being abused. Only later did I find out that two members of our squad knew, or at least had guessed, but did nothing." Quinn's fingers started to clench into a fist so he forced himself to ease up. It might all be in the past but he still got pissed when he thought about two men looking the other way when a woman had been in constant danger. After everything came out, they downplayed it, made it seem as if they weren't really sure, but screw that, Quinn didn't care. They should have said something to someone. When he glanced at Athena, her expression was soft and understanding.

She'd worn her dark hair down and washed her makeup off. She looked so damn innocent sitting there. Probably too innocent for him, but he wasn't walking away. Not again. "But *you* did something."

He nodded and ripped open a bag of shredded mozzarella cheese. He'd already done the first layer of eggplants, now it was time for the cheese and sauce layer. "Yeah, got her to a shelter and from there, the system did its job for once." Thank God. It didn't always work out that way. Of course Suzanne would have had to skirt the system in order to get a new, fake identity and he was glad she'd found those resources.

"So he went to jail for abusing his wife and what, blamed you for the fact that *he* beat his own wife?" Now Athena sounded incredulous and pissed. Her tone made him smile and when he looked at her again, her Mediterranean blue eyes were sparking with anger.

"That and..." He internally cringed. No way around telling her. "He tried to kill me. Came to my house to supposedly just talk but then attacked me with a pistol in full view of some neighbors. I disarmed him, but one of my neighbors got it on video, along with him clearly stating he was going to kill me." Quinn hadn't been sure if he should tell her, but hell, she needed all the facts, especially since Glenn had personally come in contact with her.

Athena let out a small gasp, her fingers clenching around the stem of her wine glass just a fraction harder. "How is he out of prison then?"

Quinn's jaw tightened again, but some things he had to let go. The justice system was broken and he could get angry about it, but it wouldn't change anything. "Him trying to kill me was actually a blessing. For Suzanne at least. He wouldn't have gone away for as long as he did for just spousal abuse."

"So how long did he get sent away for?"

"Six years."

She was silent a moment, watching him curiously. He swore he could actually hear her thinking. "That's how long you've been with Red Stone."

He nodded. "Yes, and to answer what you're not asking, that whole incident is why I left the police department. Well, part of the reason anyway." Quinn would tell her all the rest eventually, but it wasn't important now.

"Six years doesn't seem like a long time for murder."

"Attempted murder. He took a deal and accepted a lesser charge to avoid a trial. And the term was eight to ten years but he got out early for good behavior. That shit… ah, stuff happens all the time, unfortunately." He shook his head in disgust.

"So what happened to his wife, or ex-wife, I'm guessing now?" Athena took a small sip of her wine.

"I honestly don't know. She ghosted out of town, cut contact with anyone from her past. I think she probably got a new ID and settled somewhere far from here. Just a guess, of course, but I'm glad."

"You think he'll go after her?"

Quinn shrugged. "No. I think if he could find her, he absolutely would, but my gut says he won't." Because if Quinn couldn't locate Suzanne, then no way in hell would Glenn be able to. He didn't have the resources anymore. Suzanne had deserved a fresh start and the truth was, just moving wouldn't have saved her. Glenn would have come after her later and eventually killed her if he'd been able.

She shook her head. "That's terrifying."

"Yeah, but he fu… screwed up tonight with you. I'm on guard now, and he's not getting past me."

Athena was silent, contemplative for a long moment, but he saw the relief in her eyes. "What happened to the men who looked the other way, the ones who were with your squad?"

"They were eventually let go for unrelated issues. Technically anyway." Finished with the layering, he opened her oven and slid the glass casserole dish inside.

"Ah, so the powers that be couldn't fire them for looking the other way, but found another reason to get rid of them." Her tone was approving.

Another reason—not that he needed one—he wanted to kiss her. "Yep. They deserved it too." As he moved to the sink to wash his hands, she spoke again, and this time her voice was tentative.

"So… it's none of my business, but you opened the door earlier so I'm just going to ask. When you said you haven't gone out with anyone since me, does that mean you haven't slept with anyone else either?"

Because the two were very different things.

She didn't say the words, but he heard the silent question just the same. Grabbing a dishtowel, he dried his hands as he turned to face her. In that moment he was struck by how innocent she looked. He hadn't thought he wanted that in a woman, hadn't thought he wanted to settle down at all, but being in Athena's kitchen now… he could see getting used to this, being with a woman like her day in and day out. Hell, not like her, *only* her.

"I haven't slept with anyone else. Haven't wanted to." Confessing that took a lot more effort than he'd realized, but he was glad she knew. He wasn't done pursuing her, not by a long shot.

Her lips parted just the slightest fraction, as if he'd truly surprised her. Good. Taking a chance, he covered the short distance between them and moving slowly, reached out and tucked a few stray strands of her dark hair behind her ear.

She sucked in a shaky breath, her eyes flaring with an emotion he recognized well; lust. He wondered if she was remembering just how hot things had been between them. He hadn't been able to get her out of his head for two months. Hadn't been able to forget the way she'd looked as she straddled him in his truck, the little moans she'd made when he'd gently teased her nipples with his fingers—unfortunately over her lacy bra. She'd been so sensual, so reactive, and he couldn't get enough.

When she swallowed hard enough for him to hear, he let his hand drop.

Not because he thought she wouldn't be receptive if he kissed her. He could tell she was. Their attraction wasn't the issue. But he didn't want her to ever come back and say she'd made a decision under stress, that she regretted it. The next time they came together it wouldn't be because of a situation where they were forced together and she'd just been terrified by an asshole.

Because the next time, they weren't stopping at just kissing and he wasn't letting Athena go. Clearing his throat, he took a step back. "I'm going to grab a shower, but the timer should go off in an hour." He'd be back down before it did, but needed some distance or he was going to forget his good intentions.

CHAPTER SIX

One week later

Athena peeked through the peephole of her front door and let out a little sigh of relief to see Ivan Mitchell waiting for her. She was flying out on one of Red Stone's private jets today and he was her escort to the airport. Harrison wanted her in Vegas a day before the tradeshow started and that was fine with her.

The past week she'd practically lived at the office, mostly because of work, but she'd also been taking all her lunches in the lobby deli because of 'the incident' as she'd begun to think of it. She'd literally just gone from home to work and back again. Since the past week had consisted of a lot of conference calls and other types of planning that she could work on in-office, the schedule had been fine. But it wasn't a long-term option and she wasn't screwing up her new job because of this thing with Glenn White. If she needed to meet a potential client out for lunch—which she knew would happen often—she was doing it.

On top of everything else, she'd spent one night at her parent's house because her mom had freaked out when Stephanos—the traitor—had broken down and told her about what happened. Not something Athena wanted to repeat any time soon. Whenever she went home her parents treated her like she was twelve. To top it off, *all* her sisters were in high school now so it was constant World War III drama over there. Thankfully she, with Belle and Grant's help, had managed to convince her mom that she was fine to move back home. Athena would have left regardless, but it was nice that her cousin helped smooth the way.

Glenn White hadn't made any more contact with Athena and none at all with Quinn. Since White hadn't done anything illegal the police weren't involved. That didn't mean Quinn wasn't in a sort of protective overdrive mode. Which she understood, but she couldn't let her life revolve around something that may or may not happen. And he'd wanted to stay over too, but after that first night she'd had to say no. She had a security system—literally the best since it was from Red Stone's very small residential department—so no one was getting into her house. Plus Quinn and Grant made her check in with them every night and every morning. Overkill, but not the worst thing in the world to have people care about you.

Quinn had also been texting her and doing daily drop-ins to see her at work, but she'd been trying to keep things professional between them. It was so hard though, especially since he looked at her with a simmering lust that always got her flustered.

"I just need to set the alarm," she called out to Ivan.

"Okay."

She set it to away mode, then opened the door. Before she could think about protesting, the huge Viking-looking man picked up her suitcase and carry-on with a grunt. "You got freaking bricks in here?"

"Ha, ha." She shut the door behind her and locked it. "Something tells me Julieta packs a lot more than me." His adorable fiancée was a fashion plate. The woman owned a local shop that sold lingerie and sex toys and always looked so put together. Julieta was a few years older than her, but Athena had gone to high school with one of Julieta's younger cousins. Small freaking world.

"You wouldn't be wrong. She told me to tell you hi, by the way."

"Tell her hi back." Athena slipped her keys into her purse, feeling like she'd forgotten something even though she'd triple-checked everything. "You ready for Vegas?"

"There's been a change of plans..." He trailed off as his phone rang.

While he answered, she plucked her carry-on bag from where he'd set it down and slid it into the back of the open-hatch of the SUV.

He made a sound of annoyance, but she ignored him. She'd traveled on her own for two years and didn't expect anyone to carry her bags for her. He was faster than her with the bigger bag so she got into the back seat and pulled her tablet from her giant purse. She didn't recognize the driver but smiled at him before turning on her tablet. She could at least check her email before they took off.

At this point Athena had everything for tomorrow's event pretty much lined up but she was supposed to meet with Iris Christiansen early in the morning. Iris was head of The Serafina's hotel security—and was also the wife of billionaire Wyatt Christiansen. Athena knew the woman had once worked for Red Stone, and if she was being honest, she was a little intimidated to meet her. Whenever she'd heard any of the guys talk about Iris, it was with respect.

Ivan was still on the phone by the time they reached the private airport, going over what sounded like last-minute security additions to another job.

"Sorry about that. Didn't plan to be on the phone the whole drive," he said as they pulled up on the tarmac. "Blue's keeping me here this week, but Harrison wanted a familiar face to escort you to the airport."

It took Athena a moment to figure out who Ivan meant but then she remembered that Alexander Blue was Ivan's more-or-less direct boss. Blue ran one of the southeast divisions of Red Stone. There were so many names to remember but she thought she was doing a pretty good job so far. "No problem, work's work." Now real energy hummed through her at the prospect of handling her first real job for Red Stone. Raegan wouldn't be flying out until Tuesday, so tomorrow and most of Tuesday, Athena was on her own.

When the driver grabbed her bags, this time she didn't protest, just walked with Ivan to the waiting plane. She was surprised she didn't have any security with her since Harrison had made it sound like a team would be going, but maybe they were coming out Tuesday with Reagan.

Too excited about the job to be worried, she nearly stumbled when she stepped inside the plane to find Quinn standing next to a table where Travis sat looking at his laptop.

Concealing her surprise—and that burst of pleasure that detonated inside her at seeing him—she moved farther into the interior of the sleek plane. "Hey, I didn't realize you two were coming with me."

Travis spared her a quick smile and a nod, but didn't stop whatever it was he was doing. From his intense expression she guessed it was work related.

"Last minute change of plans," Quinn said smoothly, turning so he faced her fully.

There was something in his gaze she couldn't quite define, but it made her heart rate kick up just the same. After his revelation on Monday night about not having slept with or dated anyone since going out with her, she wasn't sure how to act around him. It was unnerving, reminding her of being in high school and feeling so damn unsure of herself. He'd really messed with her heart by ending things because of something that seemed so trivial, but she couldn't deny that the past week she'd started to fall for him again. Okay, maybe there was no 'again'. Just sort of a continual thing. "Oh."

"Don't sound too excited." His voice was wry now, those midnight dark eyes of his assessing.

Her lips curved into a smile. "I didn't mean it like that."

He started to respond when his gaze flicked over her shoulder. She turned to find the pilot and flight attendant—who looked like brothers—moving into the cabin with instructions about how they needed to sit for weight distribution and get ready for the flight.

Moments later Athena found herself seated next to Quinn—who smelled far too good—with Travis across the aisle from them. He'd closed his laptop and pulled out earbuds, and surprisingly, a sleep mask. Travis glanced at them and held up the mask. "Little man didn't sleep well last night so I'm going to catch a few Z's on the flight."

Athena could imagine—though didn't want to think about having kids for a long time—and nodded back. As the pilot's voice came over the speaker and the flight attendant moved past them to the back, she leaned back in her seat to the soft rumble of the engine starting. She'd been on so many flights over the past two years, including on private planes, and usually found take-offs almost cathartic.

Not today. Not sitting next to Quinn who was semi-casual in black slacks and a gray sweater that she was pretty certain was cashmere pushed up to his muscular forearms. Seriously, why did forearms have to be so sexy?

Why did *he* have to be so sexy? And why did she have the ridiculous urge to reach out and stroke his... sweater. She just wanted to see if it was as soft as it looked.

Right. She snorted at the thought then cringed as she saw Quinn glance at her out of the corner of her eye. She hadn't meant to do that out loud.

Half-smiling, she looked at him. "So Harrison gave you this last minute, huh?"

He paused for a moment, his dark eyes unreadable. "I requested the job."

Ah, okay then. She so absolutely did *not* know how to respond to that. She'd told him last week that there was no chance between them. But there had been that weird sexual tension between them in her kitchen the night he'd stayed over. She'd been so sure he would kiss her, but at the last minute he'd reversed course and left her pretty much panting for more. Because she certainly wouldn't have rejected him.

He wasn't pressuring her or anything, but he was just being so... honest about stuff. Why had he requested this job? Either he was worried about her because of White or he'd requested it because he wanted to work with her. Or maybe it was a combination of both.

She wasn't asking why though. Instead she decided to ignore the fluttery feeling in her stomach and stick to a safe topic. "Have you been to Vegas before?"

He shook his head. "Nah. Never wanted to, but I've heard The Serafina is amazing. You been?"

"I'm a first-timer too. And from the pictures I've seen, the hotel and casino really are amazing. Is there anything extra we need to go over for the tradeshow?"

"Once we get settled in we'll do a walkthrough of the tradeshow area and talk to all the onsite staff to get a feel for the layout, but I think we're good for now. I read over your files. Very detailed." A ghost of a smile teased those very kissable lips.

She had to resist the real—and again, ridiculous—urge to lean in and brush her lips over his. He was making her feel out of sorts and she couldn't deal with that. Not right now. "Good, that's my plan too. Did you ever work with Iris Christiansen before?"

"Yeah. She's the best. Very professional." Another smile touched his lips and this time she saw humor in his eyes.

"What is it?"

"Just thinking about the last job I worked with her. It was long before she married Christiansen and moved to Vegas. One of our clients—now an ex-client—thought he could get handsy with her. Before anyone on the team could move she had that guy flat on his stomach with one hand wrenched behind his back and was reaming him out with language that uh, could make a sailor blush. Working with her was always entertaining."

Feeling more at ease, Athena settled back against her seat as the flight attendant approached them, asking if they wanted anything to drink. After requesting a bottle of water—she'd learned to stay hydrated when traveling—she reclined her seat a bit more and decided to turn off her brain for the flight. Soon enough she'd be working her butt off and spending plenty of time with Quinn.

That thought excited her way more than it should have. She was the one who'd said no to more with him, but just being in such close quarters with Quinn was short-circuiting her brain. Despite that, he still made her feel safe, secure. Even though White hadn't reached out again she still liked knowing Quinn was nearby right now.

* * *

"I don't know how you made a tradeshow room about GPS and transportation not boring, but everything looks pretty great," Travis said as they got on the elevator to head up to the executive floor.

Their bags had been taken when they'd arrived at the hotel hours ago and they hadn't been to their rooms yet. And Athena didn't know that she was sharing a suite with Quinn. Something he knew was going to annoy her, but it was happening. He was still wired about Glenn. Didn't matter that they were across the country, Quinn took Athena's safety seriously. And yeah, he wanted to open up the opportunity for more to develop between them.

Since they'd have two separate bedrooms with an adjoining living room area, it was basically like they had separate rooms. He didn't think she'd see it that way since Travis would be across the hall, but she'd just have to deal with it.

"That wasn't me, it was a local design firm who set everything up," Athena said.

"You hired them and approved everything," Quinn said, pressing the button to their floor.

She shrugged. "I'm pretty sure this is going to be one of the more fun tradeshows I've done. Everything's set up ahead of time and there's no take down from day to day which will ease a lot of headaches—and how cool was that multi-tiered tire cake?"

Travis nodded, grinning as the elevator arrived on their floor. "I say we see if someone can save us some food tomorrow. The spread the catering staff already has set up is sick."

Quinn just shook his head. "We're in Vegas, and The Serafina has world famous restaurants."

"I want some of that cake."

"I'll make it happen," Athena murmured, laughter in her voice as they all stepped out.

Quinn had already pulled out his room key and handed Travis his as they approached the suite numbers. "Your bags should already be in your room," he said to Travis.

"Thanks. I want to Skype with Noel for a bit so I'm going to do room service. See you guys at six, right?"

Athena nodded as Quinn said, "Yep, meet you right out here."

"So where's my room?" she asked as the door shut behind Travis.

Quinn tilted his head at the door directly across the hall and slid the key card into it. He held the door open. "You and I are sharing a suite."

She stopped, eyebrows raised. "Excuse me?" Anger punched off her so sharply it was almost a tangible thing.

That probably shouldn't have gotten him so hot, but damn, she looked good angry. "Two separate rooms, two bathrooms, we just have a common living area." But there was only one exit. Which meant if someone wanted to enter the room, they had only one way to do it. "No one's getting past me."

She eyed him for a moment, her gaze narrowing. "Did you request this?"

"Yes."

For a moment, she looked as if she might snap at him, but just as quickly pushed out a sigh. "You are so maddening, but I'm too tired and too hungry to argue with you," she said as she strode past him. The sway of her ass was enough to make his entire body react.

He inhaled her subtle tropical scent as she moved. He wasn't sure what kind of perfume she wore, but whatever it was, or if it was just something that was intrinsically Athena, it drove him crazy.

She drove him crazy. Ever since their 'almost kiss' a week ago in her kitchen he'd been going out of his mind. Well, *more* out of his mind for her. Especially since he already knew what she tasted like, how she felt in his arms. "No argument at all?" he asked, trailing after her, but not before engaging the locks and security bar.

"If you really want an argument I might be able to build up some steam," she murmured, entering the huge living area. "Holy crap this place is huge. For past jobs I usually got the basic room. Nice, but boring. This…" She glanced over her shoulder at him as he moved to stand next to her. "This is beautiful."

He nodded in agreement, taking in the living area in one sweep. The silver and purple drapes had been pulled back to reveal the sparkling city below. A circular, ornate table sat in front of a huge half-circular shaped white couch. A gift basket with an assortment of food and champagne sat on the table. On another two tables by the window were huge vases of what he was certain were fresh flowers. Purple roses to go with the rest of the room.

"Give me a second to sweep the bedrooms," he said, though he was certain they were secure. This floor was one the owner reserved for business associates not necessarily in town to gamble, or for extra security personnel like him. It was more or less a private floor.

When he returned to the living area he found Athena had already opened a box of crackers from the gift basket and was cutting a block of cheese. "Want a snack?" she asked, smiling at him.

He wanted a snack all right. With the city lights illuminating her from behind, he thought she certainly lived up to her namesake. She'd taken off her fitted black jacket and high heels—which he knew she hated wearing anyway—and stood there in a slim-fitting black and red dress that hugged all her curves. He wanted to slowly peel off her clothes and feast on every inch of her delicious body. He'd only seen her partially unclothed when they'd been dating but he'd fantasized about what she'd look like completely bare to him.

Before he could respond there was a knock at the door.

Without thought he pulled out his weapon, ignoring her little gasp of surprise, and strode for the door. A glance through the peephole eased his tension though, and he pulled the door open for Iris as he sheathed his pistol.

The tall, darker skinned woman with clear Native American heritage gave him a small smile as she held out a hand for him. "Quinn, good to see you."

He nodded, shook her hand then stood back so she could enter. "You too. Everything okay? We were told you were off site today for something."

"Yeah, got back a little while ago and wanted to meet Miss Manikas in person. I like what she's done with the..." She trailed off as Athena strode into the tiled entryway, her heels clicking quickly as she approached.

Quinn wasn't surprised she'd put her shoes back on and though he knew she didn't like the heels, he'd had more than one fantasy involving her wearing them and nothing else. Something he did *not* need to be thinking about right now.

"Miss Manikas." Iris, who had a hard edge, gave her a surprisingly warm smile. "You look so much like Belle."

Athena blinked in surprise as she approached, took the hand Iris had offered, and returned the smile. "Call me Athena, please. I didn't realize you knew my cousin."

Iris nodded. "Yep. Did more than my share of jobs with Grant. And call me Iris. I just wanted to stop by and meet you in person before the madness of tomorrow—and this week."

Quinn was silent as the two women chatted, struck by the physical differences of them. Where Iris was tall, lean and had a fierceness to her he'd only ever seen in military or law enforcement individuals, Athena was petite, so open with her expressions and had a softness to her he found irresistible. For some reason he knew she'd hate that term, but there it was.

Once Iris left, Quinn locked and secured the door behind her to find Athena taking off her heels again.

"I'm going to grab a shower and probably crash," she said, heading back for the main area.

He barely bit back a groan. She was going to be naked soon with steam billowing around her hot little body, water rushing over her soft skin—fuck him, he needed to get his thoughts under control. He cleared his throat. "I was going to order room service. You sure you don't want anything?" It had been a long day.

"Nah, I'll just grab some fruit from the basket. But will you order breakfast tomorrow for us when you call for room service tonight? I know what I want."

"Sure." As he strode to the room's phone, his cell buzzed in his pocket, indicating a text. When he saw the message on screen from Grant, his chest tightened for an instant, but he kept his expression neutral.

White slipped our guard. Knew he had a tail. Could mean nothing, but he hasn't been back to his place all night. Also found something interesting. Can't text. Call when you're free.

"Everything okay?" Athena asked, barely glancing up from where she was picking through the fruit in the basket.

"Yeah." But he knew it wasn't. Grant wouldn't have texted otherwise.

Quinn knew that Grant had broken into White's apartment earlier today. Illegal as hell, but Athena was Grant's family. The truth was, if Grant hadn't done it, Quinn would have himself. There hadn't been a chance this week. So the text meant Grant had found something inside the apartment. Something he couldn't put in text form. No way in hell would Quinn ever tell Athena either. She didn't need to know what her cousin-in-law had done for multiple reasons. One being plausible deniability.

Quinn shot off a quick reply to Grant telling him that he'd call in a few minutes. As soon as he had privacy. It seemed a slim possibility that White would come after him while he was in Vegas, but with Athena here, Quinn wasn't taking any chances with her safety.

Whatever it took, he'd protect her.

CHAPTER SEVEN

Glenn vibrated with an urgency he hadn't felt in years as he handed the cab driver the cash. Once he got his change and tipped the guy the expected amount he slid out of the vehicle, duffel bag in hand. He kept the gratuity dead-on average. Not too cheap, but not too flashy either because he couldn't afford to stand out, for anyone to remember him. Bright neon lights glittered everywhere, people talking, laughing, stumbling along the sidewalk as they made their way to their destinations. The energy of the city was invigorating.

No longer was he just surviving day to day, keeping his head down and making sure he maintained his 'good behavior'. Now he finally had a chance to pay back the bastard who'd been the catalyst in his imprisonment. More than that, the one who'd taken Suzanne away from him.

The more Glenn thought about it, the more he realized that Quinn had to have helped Suzanne leave. It was the only thing that made sense. Since he'd helped her, he'd know where she was now. Under normal circumstance he didn't think Quinn would tell him where his unfaithful wife was, but now that Glenn had formulated a plan he knew Quinn would.

Glenn had called in every favor owed to him—mainly old CI's or criminals he'd let slip through the cracks—and through different sources he'd first discovered that the woman he'd seen Quinn with was named Athena Manikas. He thought he'd nailed down her address but it turned out to be old. Unless she had a sixty-year old black grandfather for a roommate, because that was the only person he'd seen coming in and out of her listed place of residence. That was okay though, he'd expected hurdles.

It didn't matter anyway because he'd just hit the jackpot with news that Quinn and the Manikas woman were both in Vegas. One of his contacts had tracked use of both their credit cards to the same hotel; The Serafina.

Coming to Vegas had been a huge risk, but he'd already checked in with his parole officer and she was just another malleable woman. She didn't care about him as long as he didn't cause any trouble. He had another five days before he needed to check in with her again and all he had to do was make a phone call. Didn't even need to visit her in person unless she requested it. And she never did. Wasn't like she tracked his phone—not that he'd brought his regular cell phone with him anyway. Lazy bitch.

February was cold in the desert and he liked the cool air rushing over him. Made him feel alive. Hell, he felt alive for the first time in six years, two months. Tugging his ball cap low on his forehead, he didn't feel out of place wearing sunglasses at night as he strode down the busy strip. Tons of other people had on sunglasses this late too.

No one was paying attention to him. No one cared that he was here. Soon Quinn was going to, though. That bastard was going to care a whole lot.

Once Glenn took Athena, threatened to hurt her—did hurt her—Quinn would tell him everything he wanted to know. It would probably only take a few slaps, punches, maybe he'd have to use a blade on her. Maybe not. It all depended on Quinn's willingness to talk. Glenn would still kill them both once he got Suzanne's location, but he wouldn't make the smart-mouthed bitch suffer if Quinn was straight with him. He'd give him that much. Glenn couldn't say the same for Quinn though.

He was going to hurt him before he died. They'd both worn a uniform, served together; Quinn shouldn't have ratted him out. It went against their unspoken code. Once Quinn was dead too, Glenn would bury him and his woman in the desert. If things got too hot for him he'd flee to Mexico, but if he did this right no one would even know he'd been here.

When The Serafina came into view, a sleek high-rise shimmering against the night sky, Glenn smiled. All the rage and anger that had been simmering inside him for years pushed at the surface, ready to break free.

Ready to make Quinn pay for what he'd done.

* * *

"You didn't eat enough today," Quinn murmured next to her.

Athena didn't open her eyes though. She had her head leaned back against the interior of the elevator and was close to passing out on her feet. The subtle vibration from the elevator was going to make her fall asleep faster if they didn't make it to their room soon. "Were you keeping tabs on me?"

He just made a grunting sound.

When the soft ding sounded, she opened her eyes and breathed out a sigh of relief. "I'm wearing lower heeled shoes tomorrow," she said as they stepped out into the hallway.

"And eating more."

She just shook her head. She'd been too nervous to put away much. Plus, and she knew it was her own issues, being around Quinn so much made her very aware of her weight and size. Around him she felt small and petite, but then an Amazon-beauty would make their way to Quinn, all smiles and big breasts right in his face, and those stupid insecurities flared back to life. She'd been busy today, but not so busy that she didn't notice all the women who'd gone out of their way to approach Quinn. It made her remember how chubby she'd once been and feel as if he was out of her league. She didn't like being that person, but there it was.

"I have a surprise for you." His voice dropped an octave as they reached their door.

Despite the shiver that rolled over her at his sensual tone, she shook her head. "Unless it involves a massage and a hot bath, not interested." As soon as the words were out, she wanted to snatch them back. Realizing what that had sounded like, her eyes widened as she glanced at him.

Wicked grin in place, he just slid the key in the lock and opened the door for her. "Unless you're inviting me to join you in the shower—and for the record I wouldn't say no—I hired someone from the hotel to give you an hour massage."

For once in her life she was stunned speechless. She was definitely going to go back to the part about him not saying no, but... "You hired someone to massage me?" Her heels clicked loudly against the tiled entryway.

"You looked like you could use the break after today." For a moment he looked impossibly insecure. "I... shit, was that too presumptuous? I just wanted to do something—"

"No! It's really nice. No one's ever done anything like that for me before. Thank you." She felt her cheeks heating up under his intense stare and tried to think of something halfway intelligent to say, but her brain had gone completely haywire. He'd hired someone to massage her? That was too sweet for words. Maybe it could have come off as too much, but she could tell Quinn had done it from a good place. And something told her he'd paid for it himself, not put it on the room.

"Athena?" A female voice made her turn. A tall, broad woman in scrub-like clothing and her hair pulled back in a tight bun smiled warmly at her. "I'm all set up if you're ready."

"Ah, yeah, just a second." She glanced back at Quinn, who was giving her what she thought of as his 'hungry look'. "Thanks," she murmured again. He was really making it impossible to even want to keep her distance.

He just nodded. "I'll order us room service."

She certainly wasn't going to argue about that. After the exhausting day she'd had, she was going to enjoy this gift and then dinner with him. And maybe… more. She did a mental head shake. She was way too twisted up over Quinn and right about now she was having a hard time remembering why she'd wanted to keep things professional between them. It wouldn't hurt to indulge just a little, right?

* * *

Quinn stood by the oversized window looking out over the bright city, but he wasn't really seeing anything. All he could seem to focus on was that Athena was in her room right now, getting rubbed down by someone.

He wanted to be that someone. He's specifically asked for a female massage therapist because no way in hell was he actually hiring some guy to touch her. And yeah, he knew that made him a total caveman, but whatever.

He just wished he was the one gliding his oiled hands over her smooth skin.

When someone knocked on the door, he automatically tensed and went to reach for his weapon, but stilled his hand. He'd ordered room service since he knew Athena was too tired to want to go anywhere. He'd seen the exhaustion clearly in her eyes and her body language as soon as they'd entered the elevator.

He couldn't help being tense though, not when according to Grant, White still hadn't returned to his apartment. Not to mention the freaking pictures Grant had found of Quinn and Suzanne in one of White's drawers. Just a couple and it wasn't illegal. But Grant said it appeared as if there'd been more pictures and newspaper clippings taped up in his closet. There were bits of tape and partially ripped photographs still remaining on the wall, but it didn't prove anything. And Grant had been in the guy's apartment illegally anyway so he couldn't report it.

If they decided to push with White's parole officer to check on him, they'd have to have a good reason and right now they had nothing solid. It was the waiting around for something to happen that had Quinn going nuts. Especially since White was unaccounted for. But Lizzy had done her magic and hadn't been able to find any recent credit card use or any travel records. That didn't mean anything other than White hadn't taken a commercial flight anywhere and was probably just using cash. So the fucker could be anywhere.

Keeping his weapon holstered, he checked to make sure it was room service before opening the door. As he was ushering in the server pushing a rolling cart, the massage therapist made her way out of Athena's room. Making casual small talk, he tipped both the therapist and server before seeing them to the door and securing it.

He knocked on Athena's door lightly and when she opened it a moment later wearing one of the thick white hotel robes loosely belted around her waist, he swallowed hard. Her hair was down and tousled and her eyes had a sated gleam to them. She looked relaxed and sexy and all he could think about was seducing her right there.

Wordlessly she took a small step toward him, that glint in her gaze flashing with lust. He wasn't sure if she was even aware of the tiny movement, but he wasn't backing down unless she told him to. He was already rock hard with wanting her. Hell, he seemed to stay in that perpetual state whenever he thought about her.

Tired of waiting, he closed the short distance between them. She stepped forward as he did, her intentions clear. Sliding his hand through her dark hair, he crushed his mouth over hers. She moaned as she arched into him, not even pausing in her reaction.

Hell yes.

Greedy for more, he fisted her hips and hoisted her up against him. Without pause she wrapped her legs around him, her robe easily splitting open.

His heart thundered in his chest as he grasped the back of her head. Her tongue danced against his in a fervent rhythm. It had been like this before with them, the need to taste her, to touch her, so overwhelming he felt practically possessed by it. The only difference this time was that he wasn't backing down or walking away.

He didn't move them far, just backed her up against the open door. It thumped slightly against the wall under their weight. Her fingers tightened on his shoulders, her short nails digging into him as she held on tight. He wished there wasn't a barrier between them, that he could feel those fingernails on his skin, that he could see and taste all of her.

His hand actually shook as he reached under the lapel of her robe, wanting to feel more of her. The second his hand cupped her full breast, she let out a little whimper and bit his bottom lip.

The unexpected sting of her teeth had him rolling his hips against her. His cock was heavy between his legs, pulsing with need and desperate to be inside Athena. He wanted to be her first... Her only. That thought sent a sudden jolt through him, but he accepted it. Nothing else to do. Athena had him all twisted up in knots and he wasn't going to fucking analyze it.

He lightly pinched her already hard nipple. She shuddered.

"More," she demanded, her voice ragged.

He slid her robe off her shoulders and she tensed as it pooled around her waist. Pulling back just a fraction so he could look down at her, he needed to see that she wanted this. Hell, he needed to hear the words.

"You want to stop?"

"No." Her answer was immediate, but he could sense hesitation there. Just a flicker of it in her blue eyes.

Not exactly surprising. Maybe it was the thought of being completely naked in front of him. He didn't know, he'd never been with a virgin before. And they'd never had a conversation outlining how much fucking experience she actually had. The farthest they'd gone was him taking her top off and caressing her over her bra. "Tell me if and when you want to stop." God, he wanted inside her though.

She nodded, her eyes a little wide, her chest rising and falling faster than normal. Okay, she was nervous, he could see it. So he left the robe pooled slightly around her waist, held up by the belt so that just her breasts were revealed.

They were perfection. *Compliment her*, his brain shouted at him. "I've been fantasizing about kissing these for two long months," he murmured. Pale brown nipples tipped pert, full breasts.

She let out a little gasp at his words, but he didn't give her a chance to respond. There was no need to and he was too damn greedy for the taste of her now anyway. Groaning, he dipped his head, sucking one bud into his mouth.

He heard more than saw her head fall back against the door. She arched up, pushing herself farther into his mouth. While he flicked his tongue over the bud, he cupped her other breast, teasing her nipple with his thumb in slow, lazy circles.

She squirmed against the door, her legs tightening around him in a harder grip. Continuing to flick his tongue over her in teasing strokes, he reached between their bodies, sliding the robe out of the way to cup her mound. He'd expected to have to push material out of the way but she wasn't wearing anything under her robe.

He felt the softest bit of hair on her mound as he slid a finger along her slit. Wet. So fucking wet.

Sucking in a breath, he drew his head back. "This for me?" The question was practically a growl. He knew the answer but wanted to hear it, was desperate to.

Her cheeks tinged pink but she gave him a small smile. "Yes. I thought about you while I was getting my massage too."

For a long moment his brain seemed to stutter before jerking back to life. "You wanted *my* hands on you instead?"

A quick nod, her breathing growing even harsher. The rise and fall of her chest was erratic now.

His throat tightened as he thought about her stretched out on the massage table, thought about smoothing his hands up and down her entire body, over her sweet curves, between her legs. He curled a finger inside her damp heat at that thought and her eyes went heavy-lidded again.

He loved seeing that expression on her, so relaxed and sensual. He shouldn't be surprised by how tight she was, but damn. Slowly, he moved his finger deeper, savoring the feel of her clenching around him.

His cock pressed painfully against the zipper of his pants but that was too damn bad for him. They wouldn't be doing everything he wanted tonight because it was too soon for her. He was going to learn more about her body, what she liked. Because he was going to feel her coming against his fingers or mouth tonight. Maybe both.

Keeping his hand right where it was, cupping her, he set her feet on the floor and knelt in front of her.

Her eyes widened slightly until he took his free hand and slid it up her ankle and calf in a caress. Her skin was smooth but he felt the goosebumps as he moved higher. That hint of nervousness was there again, but there was a heavy measure of trust in her eyes. One he wasn't going to betray.

He'd fucked up once, but if she trusted him with her body, he'd never betray that. Without much encouragement, she lifted her leg, seeming to know exactly what he wanted her to do. She propped her heel on his shoulder, opening herself up to him in the sexiest way. Part of him wondered if she'd ever done this before, if even this would be her first time too.

The scent of the tropical oils the masseuse must have used combined with Athena's sweet scent. It was damn near overwhelming. Just like everything else about her.

He looked up, seeing the mix of hunger and hesitancy in her expression. Soon, all she'd feel was pleasure. He'd make sure of it. Inhaling that sweet scent, he leaned forward and covered her clit with his mouth, lightly sucking on the nub without any buildup.

"Quinn," she gasped out, her hips rolling against his face.

He moaned, loving the sound of his name on her lips, especially under these circumstances. He hoped she felt the vibration of his moan, that it combined with the strokes of his tongue. If the way she was moving her hips against him was any indication, he'd hit a good rhythm.

Sliding his finger deeper inside her, his cock jerked as she tightened around his digit. The thought of thrusting inside her, filling her with more than a finger had all the muscles in his body pulling taut. He imagined how tight she'd be, the sounds she'd make—

"Quinn, oh hell, I'm coming." Athena's words were rasped out, the rolling of her hips growing faster and more unsteady against his face.

Yes.

He pushed his finger deeper into that slickness. She bucked against him again. He sucked on her clit with more pressure than he'd used so far.

Her inner walls clenched convulsively around his finger as she found her release, her orgasm seeming to go on forever as she let out gasping little moans and gripped his head with her fingers. As if she thought he might stop what he was doing or maybe just to support herself.

Eventually her climax ebbed, but he felt the little flutters of her pussy around his finger. And felt like a fucking caveman, all proud he'd made her climax. He didn't know if he was the first man to have pleasured her like this and a couple months ago he might have said he didn't care. But fuck that, he hoped he was. He planned on giving her a lot more orgasms. Next time he wanted to see her face though, wanted to see those blue eyes as pleasure pulsed through her. Wanted to see her expression as he pushed inside her.

Her fingers loosened their death grip on his head and she sagged against the door as he pulled back. Though he hated to, he withdrew his finger and stood. His heartbeat was an erratic rhythm in his chest.

Her smile was slow, her expression completely satisfied as she looked at him. No regret there. Then to his surprise, she reached for his belt, tugging the buckle free as she kept her eyes pinned to his.

Unsure exactly what she planned, he placed his palms on the door on either side of her head and let her have her way. If he touched her now he was likely to hoist her up against the door and strip the rest of her robe completely off. But he didn't think that's what she wanted.

Slowly, she tugged his zipper down, then broke her gaze from his as she shoved his pants just a bit down his hips. He was dying with the need to feel her hand around him. Another grin teased her lips. "Boxer briefs.

I've wondered," she murmured, hooking her fingers under the elastic and moving them down to join his pants.

His cock sprung free, heavy and thick. Before he had time to contemplate anything, she gripped him and stroked upward. Once, twice, and he groaned at the feel of her smooth fingers wrapped around him.

"Tighter." He watched her face, saw her lips quirk up a fraction as she did just that. But she wasn't looking into his eyes, she was watching herself stroke him, as if mesmerized.

It was fucking hot.

Her grip was harder now, faster, and he was so close he should probably try to hold off. But he didn't want to. When she cupped his balls, which were pulled tight, with her other hand and tugged gently, he gave up any sense of control.

Letting go, he crushed his mouth to hers as his climax slammed into him. She let out a yelp of surprise, his kiss taking her off guard. But she didn't stop stroking.

A growl erupted from him as he emptied himself over her hands and his stomach until what seemed like an eternity later, his brain cleared somewhat.

Breathing hard, he pulled back to see Athena's face. The hint of a Cheshire cat smile was in place, her eyes dancing with too many emotions for him to sift through. He didn't think she had any, but… "Regrets?"

Shaking her head, she nudged his stomach with her hand. "No, but we need a shower."

Laughing, he nodded. He was still stunned that she'd stroked him to climax, but glad there didn't seem to be any barriers between them anymore. "Agreed. We'll take it together." Without giving her a chance to protest, not that he thought she would, he tugged the belt on her robe completely free and let it fall to the ground. It had been mostly off by now, hanging low on her hips, but to see her standing completely bare in front of him did something ridiculously primal to him. He wanted to claim Athena, wanted to let pretty much every man with a pulse know that she was taken.

CHAPTER EIGHT

Athena curled up against Quinn's chest, pleased that he'd wanted to sleep in the same bed. She wasn't exactly sure what they were, if anything, relationship-wise, but she was glad he hadn't showered then headed back for his room. Not that she'd really thought he would.

The massage and orgasm had left her feeling almost lethargic. Add in the steaming shower with the beyond-sexy man stretched out on her bed and yeah, she was feeling good. He'd washed her hair and body in the shower, which had been a new, sensual experience. Even better than her massage because it had been Quinn's hands on her.

He was completely naked but she'd tossed a T-shirt on. She wasn't used to sleeping naked and still felt a little out of her depth with him regardless of what they'd just shared.

His finger traced up and down her spine almost idly. His heart rate was too fast, as was his breathing. And she could see the bulge beneath the covers. Though her knowledge was limited, he had a very impressive cock. Next time she wanted to taste him, but now wasn't the time. Of course she didn't think he'd stop her if she started going down on him, but this quiet holding was really nice and she wasn't ready to give it up.

"So, how is it that you're a virgin?" He asked the question quietly and she automatically stiffened before she realized his tone was just curious. He proved that by continuing. "I'm not saying it's a good, bad or abnormal thing, I'm just... curious. You're a smart, beautiful woman."

Shifting against his chest, she looked up at him, wanting to see his face. Unlike the exterior room adjoining their suites, her bedroom had a jaguar print/jungle theme going on. The headboard was a fabric print with what she assumed was fake amber jewels lining the top. They glittered against the lights from the city through the sheer privacy drapes. Even though the bed was shadowed, Quinn was perfectly illuminated as well. "You first, when did you lose yours?" Not that she'd lost hers yet, but that would hopefully happen soon.

"Ah, the week I turned sixteen." He grinned almost sheepishly. "It was cliché too, with my girlfriend in the back of my car."

She let out a short laugh, relaxing at his honest answer. "Part of the reason is my family dynamics. I wasn't even allowed to date until I was sixteen and even then it was only in groups. Since I wasn't really rebellious and I went to a private school where I had male cousins in grades above and below me, even if I'd wanted to get involved with someone..." She shrugged, debating if she should tell him the real reason.

"Nothing can stop sixteen year old hormones," he murmured knowingly. When she snorted, he continued. "At least not in my experience."

She shifted again, this time rolling back over so that she was still tucked in the crook of his arm, but looking over his chest and out the window. "Okay, being completely honest, I was overweight in high school and the first two years of college. I didn't want anyone, especially a guy, to see me naked. Sex and dating just weren't a concern to me because of my own issues." She'd never told any of the guys she'd dated this truth and it was freeing.

"My third year of college I guess I semi-rebelled—according to my over-protective parents—and decided to move out of their house. I roomed with this girl who was a fitness nut. Built like a freaking goddess, no joke. Her name was Candy, also not a joke, and she was—is—awesome. She started dragging me with her to jog in the mornings using the excuse that she wanted a workout buddy. I think she just picked up on my insecurities and wanted to be a good friend. From there I started making little changes and..." Athena shrugged again, not needing to give him the breakdown of all the changes she'd made in her life. "I shed twenty pounds that year and started toning and watching what I ate."

Quinn kept stroking, his hand steady and strong. "That's impressive... though twenty pounds isn't..." He trailed off, as if maybe unsure he should continue.

She looked up at him. "It's not a lot, if that's what you're going to say, but when you're five feet, two inches, it kind of is."

"I bet you gain it in your tits and ass," he murmured, reaching down to squeeze her butt.

She blinked, taken off guard by the blunt statement. "Oh my God, you're such a guy!"

"I'm glad you noticed." The glint in his dark eyes was purely wicked. He turned his body now so that they were flush against each other, his erection pressing insistently against her abdomen.

She threw her leg over his hip, savoring the closeness. "Now that I've been honest... Why did you freak out when I told you I was a virgin?"

For a long moment, he was silent, his expression so neutral she hated it. Thankfully he answered. "It wasn't exactly that you were a virgin. But I used that as an excuse." Now he looked almost sheepish.

"Why?"

"The only real relationship I was in was back in my Marine Corps days. It didn't end well. And I take some of the blame, I'm certainly not perfect, but... she just got pissed at everything I did. Things I had no control of, like training or deployments. We fought more than anything else near the end and it was so damn tiring. Once we broke up it was like a weight had been lifted."

She nodded slightly. "Okay, I'm sort of following."

"I... I didn't think I wanted anything serious and since her I haven't looked or really even contemplated getting serious with any woman. Until you. It scared the hell out of me. And I know that sounds like bullshit, but when you told me you were a virgin, it was easy to make an excuse and end things."

"Okay. I can deal with that." When he half-smiled, she continued. "Now you get to tell me something else real about yourself. Before you said that whole thing that happened with White is part of why you left the police department. What's the other reason?"

Sliding his hand up from where it rested on her hip, he cupped her cheek, his thumb gently stroking over her skin. She liked the feel of his faint calluses.

"I got out of the Corps after six years and going into law enforcement afterward seemed like the logical next step. I started working on my degree while I was in, but it was becoming clear that the job wasn't for me even before White. I respect the men and women who can do it, but the stuff you deal with day in and day out..." He shook his head, his expression dark. "It was starting to wear on me, so when Harrison offered me a job, I took it."

She thought there might be a little more to it than that, but wasn't going to push. "So you were in the Corps six years, with the police department for two and Red Stone for six... How old are you exactly?"

The corner of his mouth curved up, the grin so ridiculously sexy it made butterflies take flight in her stomach. "Thirty-two."

"Hmm, eight year difference. Not exactly robbing the cradle, but I think I might have to rethink this whole thing between us." She kept her voice light, teasing.

He snorted and pinched her butt, making her yelp. "Think all you want, I'm not going anywhere." Oh God, his voice dropped a few octaves when he said it, sending a shiver skittering down her spine.

She wasn't exactly sure what he meant by that and she didn't want to ask. Back in Miami he'd told her he wanted to take her out again, but that didn't mean they were dating or anything more serious. And yeah, she was too chickenshit to ask him. Her dating experience was limited and if this was just a fling she didn't need it spelled out for her now. She'd ask later, she told herself. Because right now she was feeling too relaxed to let anything ruin her mood.

When he suddenly rolled over, pinning her beneath him, she was glad she hadn't asked. The feel of him stretched out over her was...indescribable. She ran her fingers over the muscles of his upper arms, stopping at his shoulders. The man was so built it was hard not to get hot feeling all that power beneath her fingertips.

He nipped her bottom lip teasingly, his breath warm against her face, his spicy scent a total aphrodisiac. As he kissed a hot path along her jawline, she raked her fingers down his back. Whatever he had in mind, she was game.

"I don't think I got a good enough taste of you the first time," he said in a dark whisper that sent a shot of hunger straight to her core.

His words left her speechless and heating up to scorching levels in seconds. She'd never had a guy go down on her before, but her female cousins had been right. It *was* amazing. This time she planned to taste him too.

She pressed against his shoulder, making him raise his head, those midnight dark eyes seeming to gleam against the backdrop of the Vegas nightlife. "I want to taste you first," she said in a rush, sure her face was crimson. At least the room was dim enough to hide her reaction. She wasn't ready for full-on sex just yet, not when things were still so new between them, something he seemed to understand without her having to say anything, but she still wanted to make him as crazy with pleasure as he'd made her.

He stilled, almost like a statue for just a moment, before he swallowed hard and rolled off her. She was under the impression that it was unusual for him to give up control like this, which made the whole situation even hotter.

"On your back, hands behind your head." She attempted to make the statement as an order, but it came out more like a shaky whisper.

Which wasn't a bad thing considering his eyes went pure molten. "Take off your shirt and I'll do it," he said after a pause. That edge to his words sent a shiver streaking up her spine.

Pausing for just a second, she did as he instructed. He'd already seen her naked and tasted her, but he still sucked in a breath at the sight of her. It did something crazy to her insides that she affected him like this. "Flat on your back."

His eyebrows raised just a fraction, but he stretched out, showing off that gorgeous ripped body. Instead of straddling him right away she drank him in.

She should have gotten her fill in the shower, but her mouth was practically watering as she raked her gaze from the hard lines and striations of his chest and stomach down to his thick cock. His upper legs were like tree trunks, all built and... her nipples pebbled tight as her gaze swept back up to his impressive erection.

His breathing was unsteady now as he watched her, those eyes heated and hungry as she settled between his legs. Right about now she was incredibly thankful for her oversharing cousins because she was feeling pretty secure in what to do. One cousin in particular—with six kids so she was clearly doing something right—had been so blunt about it when Athena had asked. *Watch the teeth unless you're being playful, wrap your fingers around the base hard and stroke with your hand as you use your mouth, and don't neglect the balls.* She'd given Athena a freaking visual with fruit—something she'd tried to erase from her memory—and had been very explicit about a massage technique but Athena wasn't trying *that* her first time.

Feeling more powerful than she imagined to have this strong, sexy man at her mercy, she lightly gripped the base of his erection and inwardly smiled as he let out an unsteady, strangled moan. Oh yeah, she could do this. And she loved that he was letting her take the reins.

Instead of jumping into it, Athena leaned down and rubbed her cheek against the head of his cock. He rolled his hips and she realized his hands weren't behind his head anymore, but gripping the sheet beneath him. His breathing was ragged, but clearly he was okay with her doing what she wanted.

She inwardly grinned at his growing lack of control, liking this side to him. She flicked her tongue over the tip of his thick length, tasted pre-come. Tasting him like this made her damper between her legs. She was turned on, but this took things to a new level she hadn't expected.

Since she'd liked it when he'd feathered kisses all over her, she decided to do the same to him. Keeping her fingers wrapped firmly around his base, she stroked her tongue up the length of him, unable to fight the pleasure that ran through her as he shuddered again.

She wanted to tease him, but she really wanted to taste all of him. When she sucked him fully into her mouth he muttered a savage curse before groaning phrases like "So fucking good" and other variations of that.

She took him in her mouth as she stroked, in and out, sucking gently then harder, seeing what worked for him. It seemed clear he liked everything she did, but harder got more of a reaction so she took that advice she'd been given years ago and stroked and sucked until he fisted a hand in her hair. Not hard, but enough to get her attention.

"Shit, Athena. I'm going to come." The words came out a growl. A warning.

She knew he was telling her to pull back so he could come on his stomach, but she was having none of that.

He quickly realized it because his grip loosened, but he didn't let go. She swallowed as he climaxed against her tongue. His fingers threaded through her hair as she finished, taking all of him until he'd dropped his hand and his body had relaxed more or less boneless against the sheets.

Grinning, and okay, feeling proud of herself, Athena straddled him and shimmied up his body until she stretched out on top of him.

Moving like a fast predator, he took her off guard and had her pinned beneath him once again. She couldn't be sure but she figured he had a bit of a dominant streak. She'd thought that back when they'd been dating, and experiencing him in the bedroom now, yeah, she could see it. She liked that he'd let her explore his body all she wanted though.

"That was incredible," he murmured, dropping kisses onto her mouth, and along her jawline again.

The man seemed to already know the nuances of her body, seemed to know exactly what she liked and needed. So when he reached between her legs to cup her mound, she wasn't sure why he pulled back in surprise.

Maybe because she was so freaking wet it should probably be embarrassing.

He slid a finger inside her, making her breath catch. She was tingling all over again, already wanting more. "This is all for me." There was a possessive note in his words that made her clench around his finger.

"Yes," she whispered.

And *that* made something dark flare in his gaze before he captured her mouth in a frenzied mating. One thing she was sure of, they wouldn't be getting to sleep for a while.

* * *

"This looks great," Athena said, scanning the food list for tomorrow. "Just make sure you replace the cucumber canapés with the cheesy canapés—the ones with the roasted tomatoes—and veggie pinwheels. Those have both been a hit so just double up." The cucumber fingerfoods had ended up getting soggy and looking all around disgusting by midday. It was almost five now and no one had touched them. No need to waste all that food or space.

The woman who worked for the outside catering company they'd hired nodded. "No problem. We're going to start breaking everything down now unless you think we should let the food sit?"

"Go ahead. If you or your boss need anything else just let me know. I've got my phone attached to me." Smiling, she patted her jacket pocket. "I'll be here for another hour at least." As the woman left, Athena turned, looking for Travis or Quinn.

Over half the vendors had already left and the other stragglers were either talking to potential clients or each other. No one had to break down anything today since the tradeshow was all week. The final day would be the crazy one, but for now things had run smoothly with only a few minor blips. Athena was running high on the adrenaline of the first day's success and everything that had happened between her and Quinn.

After fooling around last night and again this morning before their very early in-room breakfast, he'd been a little tense, almost distant, but she was ninety-nine percent sure that had nothing to do with her. She'd heard him on the phone with who she guessed was Grant when she came out of her bedroom this morning, talking about Glenn White. But Quinn hadn't told her that she needed to be worried about anything and she knew he would if they were in imminent danger. So she was putting all that out of her head even though Quinn seemed to be worried about it. Not that she could blame him.

It took a few minutes of navigating through the display tables, but she found Quinn and Travis talking to an attractive woman with dark brown hair streaked with auburn highlights. She wore a fitted black suit similar to the one Athena had seen Iris in earlier. But as far as Athena could tell she wasn't carrying a gun, so she didn't think the woman was hotel security. She probably worked here though, given the style of dress.

Travis and Quinn both nodded when they saw her approaching, though Quinn's gaze softened just the tiniest bit. The woman looked at Athena, smiled briefly, then nodded at the two men.

She touched Quinn's forearm briefly. "I'll see you in a bit." Then she was gone, her heels clicking rapidly as she hurried toward one of the exits.

Athena wasn't sure what the woman meant and wasn't going to ask—even if curiosity clawed at her. "You guys tired after today?"

They both smiled, nodded. "And starving," Travis said.

Quinn shook his head. "You're always hungry."

She let out a brief laugh, tuning out the echoing sounds of the catering staff breaking down the food display tables. "How did everything go with security?" They'd only checked in with her a few times over the course of the day. Their job had been to coordinate with The Serafina's on-site security and she hadn't interfered because that wasn't her strong suit. She knew how to make an event run smoothly, but throw in the security aspect? She'd leave that up to the pros.

They did that dual head nod thing again, making her laugh as they said "Good" almost in sync.

"If there were any issues or anything I need to be aware of for future events, just send me a detailed report. I don't even want to talk about it until I get food. You guys want to grab dinner?"

"Absolutely," Travis said, running a hand over his Mohawk.

For the briefest moment, Quinn looked uncomfortable, but then his expression went carefully neutral in a way that made her stomach twist. "I can't."

Athena blinked, waiting for him to continue, to give a reason, something. When he didn't, she pushed back the disappointment that swelled inside her. "Ah, okay." She certainly wasn't going to ask him why he couldn't or what he was doing, not in front of Travis. She looked at Travis. "Want to grab a meal here or walk around and find something?"

The two men shared a look she couldn't quite decipher before Travis slid on another easy smile. "I've been wanting to try Cloud 9 and Iris said they'd fit us in anytime."

"Sounds good to me." She glanced at Quinn. "I'll see you later then?" Ugh, she felt so awkward. They hadn't defined their relationship and she didn't want to come off as needy by asking him when he'd be back to their room. Even though she really wanted to know.

He just nodded, his expression impossible to read. "I'll see you soon."

As she headed out with Travis she hated the uncomfortable feeling twisting in her gut. This morning she'd been so sure about them, that Quinn's mood and clear edginess hadn't been about her. But what if she was wrong and he'd changed his mind about them? What if he'd once again decided that the virgin thing wasn't something he wanted to deal with?

Those stupid insecurities flared up again but she told her inner voice to shut the hell up. She needed to trust him and stop over-analyzing everything. "So you've heard good things about Cloud 9?" she asked Travis, wanting to keep her mind off Quinn for now.

"Yeah, Noel told me she'd read an article about it and I had to try it. I'm surprised they didn't cater for the tradeshow."

"They're way too busy." Athena had wondered the same thing and that was the response she'd gotten. "So what's Quinn up to? Is there a security issue I need to know about?" So maybe she wasn't exactly keeping her mind off Quinn. *Freaking sue me*, she thought.

Luckily Travis didn't seem to have a clue about her and his friend because he shrugged. "He's meeting with Margot—that was the woman we were talking to before—for drinks."

His words were like a solid punch to Athena's gut. An unwanted iciness invaded her veins, but she pasted on a smile she didn't feel. "Should one of us pick up Raegan from the airport? I don't mind if you want to kick back after dinner." Her assistant's flight had been delayed but she was arriving in a couple hours.

Travis shook his head immediately. "I'll get her. You should stay at the hotel."

The noise level in the wide open lobby of the hotel as they crossed it was surprisingly minimal. Animated yes, but nothing too obnoxious. She glanced at him. "Why?"

He shrugged, but his shoulders seemed tense. "I know it's your first big job. Anything could happen with the tradeshow and you should be on site."

He wasn't wrong, but there was something off about his tone. She didn't know Travis remotely well though so she couldn't be sure.

"If for some reason you decide to leave, you need to tell Quinn or me." Now his tone was serious.

"Ah, okay." It seemed odd, but she'd known working for a security company would be different than her other jobs. And she wasn't just doing contract work anymore so this might be a companywide protocol. She started to ask Travis but they'd reached the entrance of Cloud 9. The restaurant was considered fine-dining but there was a man in front of them wearing a Tommy Bahama shirt, linen pants and flip-flops. Freaking Vegas, she supposed, the sight making her smile.

Not that it did anything to take away from the hurt and annoyance gnawing at her gut. So Quinn was having drinks with some woman? No big deal. Except it felt like it was. He could have told her. Unless his reason for having drinks with the woman was romantic.

Her mood darkened even more at that thought and when she caught Travis giving her a curious look, she pasted on another fake smile. She was good at that.

***

Feeling smug, Glenn strolled across the lobby of The Serafina, disguise firmly in place. The beard he'd opted to use looked real and did the job of covering his facial features well. He doubted Quinn would ever imagine he was here in Vegas, but when Quinn and the Manikas woman went missing it was feasible that Glenn would be looked at as a suspect. So he'd taken all precautions. He'd left his cell phone in Miami so he didn't have to worry about his phone pinging off any towers here and being tracked. And on the very real chance that any of the cameras here at The Serafina were looked at, his face wouldn't show up on any of them because of the beard and hat. Any type of facial covering messed with the recognition software programs.

He'd even added padding to his middle so he looked as if he weighed about twenty-five to thirty pounds more. The pullover sweater he wore with jeans and sneakers was a simple attire and the sweater covered his tats so there were no visible identifying features. The ball cap and beard covered enough of his face so he'd never be identified. Yep, he'd covered all his bases.

The sight of Athena walking into a restaurant with one of Quinn's coworkers made Glenn smile, but he didn't look at them too long. He just kept making his way toward the entrance of the casino. All day he'd been in and out, coming and going as he pleased, keeping an eye out for either of his targets.

That alone sent the biggest rush of power through him. He'd seen that mouthy bitch working the tradeshow. Some kind of transportation thing going on. Tomorrow he'd go inside but today he'd wanted to get things in place.

So far he had a van that he'd bought in cash from a shady car dealer. It had been all under the table too. Glenn only needed the thing to transport Athena. After that he didn't care what happened to it. Though he'd probably burn it in the desert once he'd killed Quinn and Athena. Maybe with their bodies inside. He'd have to wipe it down first though to cover all bases. He wasn't taking any chances.

As those thoughts assailed him, he shook his head, focusing on his surroundings. He couldn't afford to get distracted now. The loud sounds of the various machines and people shouting in excitement at their wins accosted his senses as he stepped fully onto the main floor of the casino.

After the long day he'd had he was going to gamble a little then head back out and see if he could secure a place to hold Athena once he'd kidnapped her. He'd scouted a few abandoned places today, both residential and commercial, but he needed to see what they were like at night. That would make all the difference.

Tomorrow, using his new fake ID, he'd enter the tradeshow and get a feel for the layout, see what the woman did all day. He needed to look for security weak spots and when she went places alone. If he could get a handle on her schedule, getting Quinn to come to him would be easy.

Then the fun would begin.

CHAPTER NINE

Quinn was off balance, his need to get back to Athena overwhelming. But he kept his expression neutral as he stepped off the elevator with Margot onto the security floor. The fiftieth floor wasn't accessible to the general public or even most of the hotel and casino staff. Just select individuals.

"How long have you been with Red Stone?" Margot asked, placing her hand on the biometric scanner of the security area.

Glass doors whooshed open and they were immediately inundated by a steady hum of voices. Walls were covered with video screens and people in suits and headsets talked at rapid speeds. "About six years."

"That how long your guy was in jail?" she asked, motioning for him to follow her along a walkway that rounded the main security center.

"Yeah." Quinn wanted to send him right back there too.

"He'd be stupid to follow you here, but I'm glad you told us about the threat." Margot stopped in front of a closed door, rapped once.

It opened a second later. Iris smiled and stepped back. Once they moved into her sleek, not-surprisingly minimalist office, she pressed a button on a window that Quinn now saw overlooked the hub of the security area. It immediately frosted over, giving them complete privacy.

"We've got some possible matches," Iris started, stepping over to a panel of four wide screens. "But nothing more than thirty-eight percent probability, which you know as well as I do is useless. These matches might as well be Martians."

Though it punched through him abruptly, he didn't show his disappointment. "How many matches?"

She picked up a remote and flipped on the screens. "Twelve." Twelve shots of men flashed on screen, layered next to each other. He stared at all of them. The images were clear enough, but most had beards and all of them had ball caps or other style hats on—and their body types varied. Quinn couldn't tell if any of them were Glenn because he could have made changes to his appearance. No, not could have, if he was here, he definitely had. The man wasn't stupid.

She continued. "We used White's driver's license photo from six years ago and his more recent one. We've also plugged in other identifying factors like his new tattoo. But none of this does us any good if he's wearing a disguise. Anything that covers his face or eyes messes with our program. It's top of the line, but technology still has limitations. And we're not focusing on the body at all since that can be altered far too much with padding."

Jaw tight, Quinn nodded, scanning over the images again. He resisted the urge to pace. Damn it, he hated that no one with Red Stone could track White down yet. The guy had just ghosted. "I appreciate you doing this at all."

Iris nodded while Margot leaned against the front of Iris's desk. "We've checked commercial flights and car rentals and haven't found anything," she said. "So why are you certain he's here?"

"I don't know that he *is* here. But his cell phone is still at his place." And who the hell left their cell phone for long periods of time? *No one.* Not unless they had a good reason. "My guys haven't seen him return to his place for days and there's been no use of his credit cards. It's like he fell off the face of the earth."

Iris lifted a shoulder. "Maybe he just rabbited out of the country."

"If he had he would have cleaned out his bank accounts." At least that was what common sense told Quinn. Because White would have wanted to buy a new ID. He'd have the contacts, but it wouldn't be cheap. But Quinn didn't think White would just leave without wanting payback. "Bottom line, my gut tells me he's here. Or at least trying to find me and possibly Athena. White isn't just going to walk away, flee the country. He'd want to kill me first. He blames me for his wife leaving." Which was complete and utter bullshit, but there would be no reasoning with a wife-beater like

White. A man who blamed everyone else for his problems. Weak and pathetic at his core.

Giving Quinn a hard stare, Iris tapped a long, elegant finger against her chin for a moment. "I'm going to put a two-man team on Athena this week when she's at the tradeshow. They won't be in her way but they're not going to blend in either. In your suite she'll be more than secure, but with the tradeshow I think we need people specifically looking out for her during the day. I've never known you to overreact to anything and I don't want to take any chances."

Quinn breathed out a sigh of relief. He'd planned to ask and was glad he didn't even need to. "Thanks, Iris."

She shrugged in that nonchalant way of hers. "From what you've told us, in White's mind you took from him so he'll want to take from you. Not gonna happen on my watch."

Quinn hadn't come out and said that he and Athena were together, but Iris was perceptive. "Thanks. You mind sending the pictures to Travis and me? I'm going to go over everything with Athena tonight, let her know to be on guard. Even if none of these guys are White..." He glanced at the screen again, frowned. It was too damn hard to tell. "I still want her aware."

"No problem. I'm flagging my top three candidates—none of whom are staying at the casino and all paid in cash, unfortunately—because of their ears."

Quinn blinked once as understanding set in. He narrowed his gaze at Iris while Margot just shifted uncomfortably against the desk. "Are you saying what I think you're saying?" he asked.

Iris just grinned, the action a little feral. "Ears are the new fingerprints."

Yeah, he knew what kind of technology was available.

Margot snorted and pushed up from the desk. "Maybe one day they will be."

Iris sighed. "Okay, there are experts that disagree, but the Feds are using it to track people… and so are we if necessary. And that's off the record. We'll find your guy one way or another."

So she was saying exactly what he thought. "I know what the Feds have. You guys have the same technology?"

Iris patted his arm, as if amused, then turned back to the screens. "Ours is better. And since we have very good photographs of White for the program to compare, it's going to make tracking him, if he comes into our casino, much easier." She pressed a few buttons on her remote control and all but three photographs disappeared.

She zoomed in on them, placing one on each screen, leaving the fourth screen dark. The top half of the men's ears were covered with hair sticking out from their ball caps, making it impossible to get a full scan. "The other nine are pretty much a no-go if you use the ear technology alone, but I don't want to narrow your results too much since the technology is still controversial in some circles. In my opinion, and because of our experiences here using it, it freaking *works*. But..." She shrugged. "You need to have all the facts."

He knew about the technology too, how effective it was. "Send all the pictures to me. Were you able to track the three men offsite?" He figured it was almost impossible and definitely illegal, but wanted to ask anyway.

Iris shook her head. "No, but now that we're aware there could be a problem, no one's going to get past my guys. I'll let you know who I pick for tomorrow and have them attached to Athena. Unless you and Travis want to be her shadows?"

His instinct was to say yes, but he paused. Part of the reason he and Travis were here was to help Athena figure out potential security issues for any future tradeshows, get her used to thinking about both sides of the coin with events. She might not want him and Travis to guard her. "Let me ask her first." If Athena preferred Iris's guys—and Quinn trusted her to have hired only the best—then he'd deal with it. Of course he still wouldn't let Athena out of the tradeshow room without him.

That she'd just have to deal with. Because he could compromise but only within limits.

To his surprise, Iris's lips curved up a fraction. "Smart man," she murmured.

He figured he understood her meaning, but didn't comment directly. "I'm going to meet up with Travis and Athena now, go over everything, but I've got my phone on me and we'll be meeting again tomorrow morning at six to head to the tradeshow."

"Just let me know if you want my guys to shadow her or replace you on the ground. Either way they'll join you at six sharp. And, I'll send you their resumes," she added, clearly reading the expression on his face.

"Thanks." Now that he'd gotten this out of the way, it was time to come clean with Athena and tell her what Grant had found in Miami and that Glenn White was potentially in Vegas. Maybe he should have told her sooner, but he hadn't wanted to needlessly worry her.

Not when she already had so much on her plate. This was her first job with Red Stone and he knew she needed to be focused. But her safety came first and if White thought he could hurt Quinn through Athena, Quinn had no doubt the bastard would try.

When he reached his floor he immediately went to Travis's door, knocked.

A few seconds later Travis opened the door in jeans, a T-shirt and his cell phone held loosely in his hand. "Hey, I was about to do a video call with Noel, everything cool?"

"I wanted to do a run down with both you and Athena at the same time so I don't have to do it twice. Want to wait?"

Travis shook his head as he stepped out into the hall. "Nah. I felt bad lying to Athena about where you were. I hadn't planned to say anything but she asked." The door shut with a soft click behind him.

Frowning, Quinn slid his key card into his suite's door. "What did you tell her?" He moved inside, Travis right behind him.

"That you were having drinks with Margot. Figured it was better than—"

His gut tightened. "Shit." He bit back the more savage curse that sprang to mind. He'd been unsure how to act around Athena in front of Travis. He hadn't wanted to embarrass her if she wasn't ready to let people know they were together. He sure as hell wanted the whole fucking world to know but it was pretty much her first week on the job so he'd wanted to move with caution. She probably thought the worst of him now.

"What is it?" Travis asked, his voice tense as Quinn headed straight for Athena's room.

"Nothing, I'll tell you in a sec." He knocked once sharply on her door. When he didn't get an answer he glanced over his shoulder at Travis. "Move back." Because he didn't want anyone to see Athena naked or in any state of undress, not even his happily married friend.

Travis looked at him as if he'd lost his mind. "Dude, you can't barge into her room. She's probably in the shower or something."

"We're... together."

Travis blinked in true surprise. Quinn figured under other circumstances Travis would have picked up on it, but he'd been asleep on the flight over and they'd been so damn busy today. "Oh... oh, hell, she's gonna be pissed at you. Sorry man, I wouldn't have said..." He trailed off at Quinn's glare, stepped back as Quinn turned back to the door.

"Athena, it's Quinn. We need to talk." He knocked again and when there was still no response, he opened the door. Something akin to fear jumped in his throat as he immediately took in the room. Untouched, the bed was still made from the daily cleaning. The bathroom door was ajar but the lights were off. Even so, he did a complete sweep of the room. She wasn't there and her purse and phone weren't anywhere visible.

He pulled out his cell as he headed toward his room. When she didn't answer his call, he texted her. No response. And she wasn't in his room either, not that he'd thought that was a real possibility. Travis gave him a concerned look but Quinn ignored him as he called Iris.

Iris answered her phone on the first ring. "Yeah?"

"Athena isn't in her room. Can you do a security check of the place?" He knew it would be easy for Iris to do a facial search and pinpoint her in less than a minute.

"On it. Where'd she go?"

"No idea." He held the phone away from his mouth as he listened to Iris give someone orders, and spoke to Travis. "She mention anything about leaving, even casually?"

"No. I told her not to leave the hotel without one of us though." He ran a hand over his Mohawk, the worry in his dark eyes clear as they headed out of the suite, made their way to the elevators.

"Got her," Iris said, the relief in her voice clear. "She's in the Cloud 9 bar area with... She's at the bar."

Instantaneous relief surged through him as they entered the plush elevator, but... "Who the hell is she with?"

"Ah, business acquaintance of Wyatt's. Pseudo-friend I guess. I'll text him now, tell him not to let Athena leave his sight. Your girl's not going anywhere."

"Who's his friend?" Quinn demanded, something in Iris's tone making him even tenser. She was holding back information.

She let out a sigh. "Name's Rhys Martin Maxwell IV. Same monetary league as Wyatt and uh, he's into BDSM. Owns a few clubs in London." She snickered before ending the call.

"Fuck!" Quinn wanted to smash his phone against the elevator wall but shoved it into his pocket.

"What is it?" Travis was in battle mode now. "Is she here?"

"Yeah. She's fine." That was all Quinn could squeeze out. Luckily Travis didn't push him, but wisely remained silent.

Quinn was aware of his surroundings at all times, but his focus was on getting to Athena. As he reached the entrance to Cloud 9 it hit him square in the chest that he was... irrationally jealous. Or maybe not exactly that, but he was what, worried that Athena was going to be swept off her feet by some fucking billionaire in the next minute? He couldn't ever remember feeling this edgy and worried. It was unsettling.

After Travis spoke to the hostess—thankfully because Quinn didn't trust himself not to snarl at the woman—they made their way to one of the bars. It was three people deep but he didn't spot Athena anywhere.

"There she is. Oh, she's with Raegan," Travis said. "She must have taken a cab from the airport. Can't believe she didn't call," he muttered.

Quinn followed the direction his friend was looking and spotted Raegan, some dick and Athena. Okay, the guy probably wasn't a dick, but Quinn was fucking revved right now. Yeah, he knew he was being beyond irrational but his brain didn't want to listen to logic at the moment. For all his woman knew, he'd been out having drinks with someone else, right after he'd told Athena he couldn't make dinner. And Quinn hadn't given her a reason for his absence, he'd just said he couldn't make it. He knew what she was thinking right now—that he was an untrustworthy ass.

"Will you make sure Raegan gets to her room safely? Make sure she knows to meet at six tomorrow?" Quinn murmured to Travis as they made their way through a cluster of high-top tables to the roped off section of modular chairs and soft lighting. He asked because he didn't plan to stay long with Athena and he wanted to make sure Raegan was taken care of. He was pretty sure the woman was even more innocent than Athena.

"Of course. You need to wipe that rabid look off your face though."

Fuck, Travis was right. He needed to get his shit under control. He'd never been like this. Never. The Corps had trained him well. But this wasn't some mission or another job.

This was Athena, and she mattered to him more than any other woman ever had.

Raegan spotted them first and smiled brightly as she stood. "Hey, guys!" Her eyes were bright, excited. He knew she hadn't been much of anywhere in the world, much less Vegas.

Quinn smiled briefly at Raegan because hell, he just couldn't be rude to the woman, ever. Ignoring the man in the no doubt custom-made suit, he pinned his gaze on Athena.

Those Mediterranean blue eyes he could drown in watched him with a complete neutrality that sliced him to the bone. There wasn't an ounce of the sensual woman who'd come against his mouth and fingers multiple times in the early morning hours. Right now that almost seemed like a lifetime ago. He should have made things clearer this morning, should have spelled out exactly how he felt about her. What he wanted and hoped she wanted too.

"I need to talk to you about a security issue now. It's important." He kept his tone professional.

Her expression immediately morphed into concern. She stood, glancing at Raegan and Travis, then back to Quinn. "Is it the tradeshow? Should we all—"

He shook his head. "It's not the show, but we need privacy. Travis will make sure Raegan gets to her room."

"Oh, ah, okay." Athena smiled warmly at the man Quinn knew was named Rhys, then made apologies to him and Raegan before telling Raegan she'd see her in the morning but to call if she needed anything.

Quinn barely resisted the urge to bare his teeth at Rhys before possessively placing his hand on the small of Athena's back and steering her out of the restaurant. It would have been impossible to miss the way she stiffened against his touch. Maybe it shouldn't have, but it pissed him off.

"Are you sure we shouldn't have included Raegan and Travis in this?" Athena asked as they reached a set of elevators. Her voice was tight, her expression pinched.

Quinn just shook his head, not trusting his voice. He wanted to tell her right then that he hadn't been out with another woman but they were surrounded by a dozen people and no one else was hearing this conversation. Because as soon as he said what he needed to, he was staking his claim on Athena.

CHAPTER TEN

Athena could feel Quinn buzzing with energy. She was beyond annoyed with him, but if there was a security issue she wanted to know about it. Now she felt just a twinge of guilt at ignoring his call and text.

She would have worried about Raegan, but Travis would be with her. Still, she couldn't imagine what kind of security situation warranted Quinn dragging her upstairs. Especially when he'd been off having drinks with another woman.

"So what's the deal?" she asked as they stepped onto their floor. They had to wait until everyone else got off on their floors before the elevator took them to this exclusive one. She had to admit it was nice to be staying in an executive area. It was so quiet compared to the rest of the hotel and casino.

Quinn placed his hand on the small of her back again, as if he had every right to touch her. As if he hadn't been out with someone else. And yeah, she knew that it might have been work related, but then why not just tell her? His behavior had been too weird and now she figured she knew exactly why. She was just glad she hadn't slept with him.

She stiffened at the touch and the man just slid his hand farther around her waist, pulling her close. When she looked up at him, he had an odd look in his eyes. Challenging almost. "Well?" she asked, since he still hadn't answered her.

"Why did you meet Raegan downstairs?"

She blinked, surprised by his question. "Why wouldn't I meet her? She got here early and is so excited to be in Vegas. She's like a freaking kid on Christmas." Despite Athena's annoyance with Quinn, she couldn't help but smile thinking about Raegan.

Even Quinn's expression softened. "Yeah, she is. Who was the man you were talking to?"

"Who was the woman you were off having drinks with?" Athena smoothly slid out of his hold as they reached the suite door. She turned her back to him, opened the door. "And why don't you tell me what this emergency is so I can get back downstairs?" She heard him let out what sounded like a growl. An actual *growl*. It shouldn't have heated her up from the inside out, but it did.

"I wasn't having drinks with Margot."

Athena nearly snorted. "So Travis is a liar?" Her voice dripped with just a bit of saccharine sweet sarcasm. As the door shut behind them, she turned to find Quinn with a dark expression on his face. She resisted the urge to take a step back.

Growling in that annoyingly sexy way, he raked a hand over his dark, cropped hair. "No, yes, I mean, no, he's not a liar but he didn't tell you the truth."

Not stepping any farther into their suite, she faced him, hands on her hips. "And why is that?"

"He didn't know you and I were—are—together."

Were they together? Her temper flared, a bright blaze inside her. "Because if he had, he wouldn't have told me you were having drinks with another woman?"

"Yes... damn it, Athena. I didn't tell Travis we were together, because I wasn't sure what you wanted. I should have brought it up to you last night or this morning, but hell, I didn't want to screw things up between us. It's been a long time since I've been in a relationship and I know this job is important to you. It's not like I'm your boss or there's a conflict, but I wasn't sure what you wanted people to know."

Some of the steam that had been building inside her faded, but... "Okay. I appreciate that. And I don't want to keep us—if there is an us—a secret."

At that, his eyes seemed to darken even more. "If?"

There was something in that one word that sent a thrill down her spine and had her nipples pebbling against her bra cups. She didn't respond because she couldn't find her voice.

He advanced on her with two strides until she found herself pressed up against the wall of the entryway. The light was dim, casting shadows over the hard, handsome lines of his face. He didn't touch her though, but laid his hands on either side of his head as he looked down at her. His breathing was slightly erratic and there was no mistaking the gleam of lust in his gaze. It was tempered with something else she couldn't quite define though.

Her heart rate kicked up about a thousand notches so that all she could hear was the blood rushing in her ears. "Where were you earlier?" Athena hated that her question came out as a whisper.

"Meeting on the security floor with Iris and Margot—she's part of their web security team. White's unaccounted for in Miami and I'm concerned he might be in Vegas. I needed all the facts before I came to you because I didn't want to worry you unnecessarily."

Athena felt a rush of relief that he hadn't been out having drinks with another woman. She knew she should be more concerned about what Quinn said regarding White, but her initial response was one of such pure relief. She'd go back to the White situation later. "Oh."

"Oh?" Still not actually touching her with his hands, he leaned down, nipped her earlobe between his teeth. "You were mad at me," he murmured.

Feeling the freedom to touch him now, she slid her hands up his chest. "Maybe a little annoyed."

He pressed down a little harder on her earlobe before oh-so-gently raking his teeth against her neck. God, the sensation of him teasing her like that made her instantly wet. She dug her fingers into his shoulders, shuddered when he started kissing along her jaw.

"I should have told you about the potential threat," he murmured, his mouth just above hers now, his breath warm as it feathered over her. "I should have told you that I'm not going to be seeing anyone else, that I don't want you to either. This thing between us is rare. I want to give us a shot."

She melted at his words and arched a little, instinctively. She wanted to jump the man, wrap her arms and legs around him and feel him push into her right against the wall. She wanted his mouth and hands on her, everywhere. "I want to be exclusive too. I felt so…" Athena almost said annoyed again, but decided to go with the truth. "Mad at you. And really hurt." Because Quinn hadn't seemed like a liar, thankfully wasn't.

For a moment, Quinn looked as if he'd say something more but then his eyes got that heavy-lidded lustful look and she knew they'd be talking much later.

"I'm on the Pill," she blurted the instant before his mouth would have descended on hers.

His big body went impossibly still, his nostrils flaring ever so slightly as he looked at her. They were so close now she could swear she heard his heartbeat—though she knew that was just the thump of hers pounding erratically. "Have you been on it long enough to go without a condom?"

"Couple months." She'd gone on it the first week they'd gone on a date because deep down she'd known that she planned to sleep with him. Because the thought of not doing so felt almost criminal.

"I'm clean." The two words were said so matter-of-factly she knew he'd been tested.

If it had been anyone else she wouldn't have taken him at face value but this was Quinn. She trusted him. She simply nodded.

He crushed his mouth to hers. Which was just as well because there was nothing left to say. His kisses were hard, demanding. She savored the commanding way he dominated her mouth, leaving her breathless and wanting more.

Clutching onto his shoulders, she arched into him. She wanted to wrap her legs around him but her knee-length dress was too fitted. As if he read her mind he tugged the zipper down the back. Instead of letting it pool around her waist, he shoved it all the way off.

Cool air rushed over her as she stepped out of her dress wearing a black matching bra and panty set and heels. She knew that was supposed to be a man's fantasy. If the hungry look on Quinn's face was any indication then yep, it definitely was.

Taking her by surprise, he fell to his knees, his intent clear. She'd thought—well, she'd thought since she'd made it obvious she wanted to have sex that he'd have gone straight for that. She didn't mind skipping a little foreplay, she desperately wanted to experience all of him and she was already wet. So wet she trembled for him.

"Gotta taste you." The words seemed to be torn from him as he tugged her underwear off.

Those words made her melt just a little more. The need and hunger that emanated from him mirrored what she was feeling. When she stepped out of the panties, he grasped her ankle, kissed her inner calf as he lifted her foot over his shoulder. Familiar with this position by now, her inner walls tightened in anticipation of what was to come. Even the feel of his lips feathering over her leg made her shudder.

"You make me fucking crazy," he murmured, glancing up at her.

The look in his eyes was electric, scorching. She was thankful for the wall holding her up.

With his gaze on hers, he slid a hand up her leg, stopping only when he reached her inner thigh. Gently, he trailed a finger along the crease of her skin where her thigh and pussy met. He was barely touching her, but it was as if she could feel his hands on her everywhere.

She wanted to tell him to hurry up, to ease the ache between her legs, but couldn't make her throat work.

When he finally teased a finger along her slick opening, he closed his eyes for a long moment. He didn't stop what he was doing though, but pushed his finger fully inside her.

She tightened around him, automatically rolling her hips, wanting way more than just this. She couldn't ever remember being so turned on, wanting something so much.

He groaned, the sound so tortured and sensual before he leaned forward and placed his mouth on her clit.

There had been moments last night when she'd felt a little insecure, especially when he'd joined her under the bright lights of the shower and could see all her flaws, but right now all of that fell away.

Quinn liked and wanted all of her. When he slid another finger inside her, she sucked in a breath and tightened her grip on his shoulders.

He groaned against her clit as he teased her, flicking and massaging her mercilessly with his tongue. When he started moving his fingers in and out of her, curving them at just the right angle, she let go completely, her orgasm punching through her fast and sharp.

It should have been a shock how fast she climaxed, but she'd been aching for him since… well, when wasn't she aching for him? It seemed that when they were in the same room, her body just flared to life.

Even when she'd been angry at him, when he'd placed his hand on her back down in Cloud 9, then again when they'd stepped out of the elevator, she'd felt that light touch all the way to her toes. And had wanted more of it.

Now she felt his touch deep inside her, craved more than just his fingers as she came apart against his mouth. She'd fallen hard for him all those months ago and when he'd pretty much run from her, it had sliced her deep. But now she knew she hadn't made a mistake wanting, needing this man so much. "Quinn," she rasped out, unable to say anything else. It was difficult to think much less speak.

He made a satisfied rumbling sound against her clit. The vibration against her sensitive bundle of nerves nearly made her collapse. When he withdrew his fingers, another shudder of pleasure spooled through her, the after effects of her orgasm lingering.

Moving with the speed of a lethal predator, he was on his feet in seconds, his mouth over hers once again.

Not for the first time had she thought it was a sensual experience to taste herself on his lips. She held onto him, hooked her legs around his waist. She knew exactly what she wanted, knew he did too. She wondered if maybe she should be more nervous about her first time but all she felt was excitement.

In seconds he had her bra off, tossed somewhere behind them. His big palms smoothed down her ass, clutched her hard as he started walking them somewhere. Her room or his, she didn't care. Hell, she didn't care if they went right down to the floor as long as he was inside her soon.

Moments later she was aware they'd entered her room as she found herself flat on her back, the glittering lights of Vegas in the background. The bed was soft, cool under her skin. The heat surging through her now was a direct contrast.

When he paused over her, his gorgeous body covering hers—and covered by too many clothes, she practically ripped his shirt off. Luckily he seemed to be more in control than her, just barely, and managed to get it off in seconds. After he did, he pushed off her, removing all that warmth and strength.

She must have made a protesting sound because he let out a low chuckle as he slid off the edge of the bed.

"I'm not going anywhere, sweetheart." There was a dark promise in those words as he started stripping off the rest of his clothes with economic movements.

When he was naked at the foot of the bed, he looked like a perfectly sculpted statue, all defined lines and striations. And he was hers. That thought sent another one of those waves of heat through her.

She started to push up so that she was on her knees, but he moved atop her with a speed that continued to surprise her given his size. She spread her thighs for him, loved the feel of him settling between her legs with no barrier. His cock pressed against her abdomen. Just the feel of it on her skin made her smile.

She slid one hand to the back of his neck, held onto him as he looked down at her. The man was absolute perfection. She was so glad he was going to be her first, was glad now that she'd waited. No matter how things played out between them, she trusted Quinn with her body and her heart.

Lazily he cupped one of her breasts and slowly, torturously rubbed his thumb over her aching nipple in little circles. This was different from the frantic energy she'd been feeling out in the hall. She still wanted him with a wildness that terrified her a little, but she was pretty certain he'd slowed things down just a bit. For her benefit or his, she wasn't certain. But she knew that he'd given her an orgasm to get her ready for him.

"This might hurt a little," he murmured, the regret in his dark eyes warming her from the inside out. She loved how much he cared.

"I know." And she *didn't* care. Not when this was Quinn. The pain, if there was any, wouldn't last. And she was so physically active she doubted it would hurt much. At least that's what her cousins had told her.

Leaning down, he took her mouth in a tender kiss as his hand moved from her breast to her mound. She arched into his hold, her hands going around his back as he tested her slickness.

In and out, he stroked her inner walls with a sweet slowness now. She let out a groan of frustration, wanting so much more. She was tired of waiting. Trailing her fingers down his back, she grasped onto his ass.

He understood what she wanted and when he withdrew his fingers, her entire body trembled with so much pent up need she felt as if she might go into sensory overload.

She wanted to see him entering her but was too shy to ask him to shift positions. It didn't matter though, the feel of his tongue dancing with hers, his hard body covering her, was heaven. His thick cock nudged her entrance and she let her head fall back from his mouth, sucked in a breath as he pushed inside her.

He didn't pump hard, but he also didn't pause, just slid into her with one smooth thrust. She met his gaze as he filled her completely. There was a moment of discomfort that she should have expected, but it was over so quickly. All she could focus on was this beautiful man inside her, on top of her. She felt so full, so possessed by him.

She dug her fingers into his backside. "More." It was all she could manage to get out, but he knew what she wanted.

He held himself up on his forearms so that she was caged in and his gaze was pinned to hers. The look in his eyes was territorial and possessive. The sight took her breath away. He pulled his hips back and began thrusting in a slow, steady rhythm.

Her hips met his, stroke for stroke, the sensation of being filled by him too incredible for words. She could feel another release building even as she wanted this to go on and on.

His breathing grew more erratic as he pumped into her, his eyes blazing with a raw heat. Part of her wanted to look away, but there was no way she could.

"Touch your clit. Come around my cock." The words were a growl. A demand. And his expression was primal.

She didn't even pause, didn't want to. Reaching between their bodies, she began rubbing herself in that very familiar way. She knew how to get herself off. It never took long, but to have someone as sexy as Quinn thrusting into her while she stroked herself put things on a whole other level.

Her inner walls began clenching around him tighter and tighter. "Faster." The word came out as a plea. She hadn't expected to come again, but felt a climax building the faster he moved. Each stroke inside her stoked that greedy fire.

She couldn't keep her eyes open any longer, let her head fall back as the sensations of another orgasm rushed through her. Pleasure poured out to all her nerve endings as she savored the sensation of him moving inside her, filling her. She'd never felt so connected to anyone. And not just anyone, but this was Quinn. She arched into him, wanting to rub her breasts against his chest, to experience more stimulation.

Suddenly she felt his mouth clamp over the tip of her breast, suck her nipple hard. The action was so unexpected, so erotic, it pushed her over the edge.

"Quinn!" His name sounded like another plea as it tore from her throat. She slid her fingers through his short hair, clasped his head with her free hand. He flicked and teased her nipple as her orgasm continued to punch through her. The sensations of his wicked mouth seemed to prolong it.

Finally she pulled her hand free from her clit, the stimulation almost too much. As she did, Quinn seemed to let go of whatever had been restraining him.

Shouting her name, his thrusts became unsteady, rough and when he buried his face against her neck, she felt him come inside her in hot strokes. The muscles in his arms and shoulders were corded tight, his back damp with sweat. It seemed to go on forever and at the same time, not long enough.

She trailed her fingers down his back in lazy strokes. His muscles tightened under her soft touch, twitched slightly as he relaxed.

"I'm too heavy," he murmured against her neck a few moments later.

She grinned though he couldn't see her. "I like the feel of you on top of me."

He pulled back, his dark eyes gentle as he looked down at her. "You okay?"

"That was amazing."

Relief immediately bled into his eyes before he dropped a sweet, almost chaste kiss on her lips. "Give me a sec." He pulled out of her and she immediately felt a difference.

Just a slight soreness she hadn't been aware of. When he'd been inside her it had been all pleasure, but yep, she was going to feel this tomorrow. Totally worth it though.

He slid off the bed and strode into the bathroom. Seconds later she heard water running. For a moment she wondered if he was just taking a shower without her, but that seemed weird.

He popped his head through the doorframe. "I'm running you a bath. Do you like it warm, hot or scorching?"

She was touched by his thoughtfulness, but didn't feel much like moving. "I don't need a bath."

Quinn stepped fully into the doorframe now and gave her one sharp headshake. "You're getting one."

She blinked in surprise at his authoritative tone. "What?"

"This was your first time, I'm not fucking this up for you." Now he strode toward her with purpose.

An unexpected laugh broke free. The man was too sweet. "Such poetry."

He froze in place and tensed. He rubbed a hand over the back of his neck—and showed off delicious muscles she wanted to trace with her tongue. "Shit, Athena—"

"I'm messing with you. And thank you. I think a soak probably wouldn't hurt." She liked that he was actually cursing in front of her now. Which was maybe a little weird, but she liked that he was being himself. It had been sweet how he'd held back before, but this thing between them felt so real. She wanted to keep it that way, didn't want any barriers between them.

"Good." He strode to the bed then scooped her up in his arms. He brushed his lips over hers, and this time his kiss was a bit more heated than the last. She clutched onto him, deepening it until he pulled back.

He groaned, simmering heat in his gaze. "Let's get you in the bath before I lose my head."

"Maybe after the bath you can lose it." She grinned at him, loved seeing the easy relaxation on his face. They still needed to talk about the potential threat but for right now she didn't want to think about anything else but this.

CHAPTER ELEVEN

Three days later

Quinn stood by the huge window of the suite, staring out at the city below. The lights twinkled like jewels under the breaking dawn sky. It was the last official day of the tradeshow, but he'd asked Athena if she wanted to stay on an extra day so they could enjoy themselves afterward. After the call he'd just received he felt a thousand times lighter. He and Athena could actually have a good time without worrying about that fuckhead White.

At a soft rustling sound he turned. Athena stepped out of her room—their room now—dressed in fitted black pants and a red wraparound top. When he realized she wore the gold necklace he'd given to her yesterday, that possessive flare he was getting used to jumped inside him. She'd protested when he'd given it to her, but he liked seeing her wear something from him. It made him feel like he was staking a claim.

"Necklace looks good," he murmured, stepping away from the window, eyeing the three tiered chains looped around her delicate neck.

She flushed pink and gently touched one of the links. "I still think it's too much," she muttered.

They'd managed to sneak away last night for a dinner outside the casino and had gotten to walk, see some of the city. He'd seen her admiring it at one of the shops so he'd gone back later and bought it. He didn't care that they hadn't been together long, he already knew he was in this for the long haul. Seeing the pleasure on her face when she'd opened the box had made him feel a hundred feet tall. Not just the pleasure though, the pure surprise. She'd admitted that no one outside her family had ever given her jewelry before and that knowledge made the caveman inside him irrationally pleased.

Not commenting, he just wrapped his hands around her hips as he reached her and pulled her close. The slightly tropical scent rolling off her wrapped around him. He couldn't keep his hands off the woman. Just being in the same room and he wanted to hold her, kiss her. "I've got good news."

"Yeah?" She slid her arms around his waist. Since she hadn't put her heels on yet she had to look up at him.

"Just talked to Grant. One of his guys saw Glenn entering his apartment."

Athena sucked in a sharp breath. "When? Is he positive?"

A smile tugged at Quinn's mouth. "I asked the same thing. About an hour ago and Grant said unless he's got a twin—and I know he's an only child—then his guy is convinced it's him. Still, Grant's going to head down there and try to get a look." There had also been recent activity on White's credit card and cell phone, all in the

Miami area. Whatever he'd been off doing the past few days, he was home now—and far away from Quinn and Athena. That didn't mean Quinn was letting the guy off his radar but for now it was a relief not to worry about White for the next couple days.

She squeezed him tighter and laid her head against his chest. "I know we'll have to be careful when we get home but at least now we can relax the rest of the today. Well, relax being a relative word because it's going to be insane today. Maybe…" She pulled back to look up at him, her blue eyes just a little wicked. "Maybe we can stay Sunday too and get home early on Monday. I don't mind going straight from the airport to work."

As that familiar hunger surged through him, he leaned down and brushed his lips over hers. She'd been insatiable the past three days. They both had. He wasn't ashamed to admit he'd quickly become addicted to her. "I bet we don't even leave the room," he murmured against her mouth.

"What do you think room service is for?" She nipped his bottom lip playfully.

Hell yeah, he thought, deepening their kiss. The next two days were going to be amazing.

* * *

Today was the day, Glenn thought as he parked his stolen van a few houses down from his first destination. He'd been covertly watching Athena and Quinn the past few days, mostly keeping his focus on the woman. He hadn't wanted to tip his hand and if Quinn sensed eyes on him, it would make him even more vigilant. What he'd first noticed was that the woman had two guards from the hotel pretty much at all times when she was at the tradeshow.

The first day Glenn hadn't been positive they were shadowing her, but the second it had been clear. Which meant Quinn somehow knew Glenn wasn't in Miami. Not hard to figure out how. Bastard had probably cased his apartment, maybe even tracked his credit cards or phone. Quinn wouldn't mind breaking the law for his own gain. So Glenn had done the last thing he wanted to and asked his cousin for a big favor. It might come back to haunt him later, but for now it was helping him cover his tracks.

He and Henry looked like brothers, the only real difference between them was about two inches in height. But they had the same build, coloring, hair, everything. People always commented that they looked like brothers so today he'd taken advantage of it.

His cousin had agreed to go to his place to check on it and get his mail. Glenn had also asked him to buy a few things for him—with Glenn's credit card—so that when he got back home he would have groceries. Easily explainable to his cousin. Getting his cousin to use his phone was a bit trickier so he'd told him he was calling it because he couldn't remember where he'd left it. Henry answered it, telling him it was in the master bathroom on the countertop.

Which gave him an alibi in Miami for today. If he was a betting man, he'd guess that whoever Quinn had sitting on his place would report that he was in Miami. Getting back to Florida after what he planned to do would be tricky, but luck had been with him so far. He was banking on it lasting, refusing to settle for anything less. Quinn deserved to pay for what he'd done.

The neighborhood he was in was quiet enough, but it connected with a busy street. Glenn slipped from the van, thankful for the cooler February weather. His gloves, knit cap and jacket weren't out of place. His fake beard was still on, but he'd dropped the padding for this job. He needed full range of movement.

He felt a little guilty for what he had to do, since the guy he was about to kill wasn't involved in this, but getting access to the tradeshow was paramount. The security had been good but today was the last day so he knew he'd have an opening to get Athena out and away from Quinn. Or he would have one if he played this right. He'd paid a shitload of money for the right equipment to jam one of the hotel's video feeds but it wouldn't last long.

His soft-soled boots were silent as he hurried down the sidewalk. He checked his watch. Almost time.

Yesterday he'd followed the van of catering staff back to their headquarters. From there he'd waited, watched, then followed a man home who'd been at the tradeshow.

Glenn had picked a guy with the crappiest car, reasoning he'd have lax security at home. It wasn't a guarantee, but he went with the odds. Once he'd seen the guy's place, he'd sat on it for a few hours last night, just watching. No one else had come or gone so unless the guy had gotten a really late night booty call, he should be alone right now.

If not, Glenn would deal with anyone else that got in his way.

Walking briskly, he held his head high and tried to appear as if he had every right to be here. Using shadows to hide his movements, he made his way to the guy's carport. He used a moldy plastic kid's pool as cover. Glenn couldn't figure why the guy had one propped up in his carport, but he didn't really care. The guy also had dirty car parts, a fax machine that looked decades old and a rusted bicycle without wheels.

Now, he just had to wait for the man to exit. Then he'd take his uniform, force him to call in sick and... likely kill the man.

It wasn't that Glenn wanted to, but this guy was in the way of Glenn getting to his wife. Because in the end, that was all that truly mattered. He needed to make Quinn not only suffer, but to spill his guts as well. Glenn needed to see Suzanne, and Quinn was the only one who would be able to tell him where she was. That bastard had been the one to convince her to leave him, to press charges. He must have been complicit in helping her hide.

When he heard the rattle of the doorknob turning, Glenn set aside thoughts of what had to be done and took a quiet, steadying breath as he withdrew his pistol. He'd kill the guy with a knife, but for now he would use the gun as a threat. His heart rate and hand were steady.

Time to take care of business.

* * *

Athena's feet were killing her, but she didn't even care. They were in the last stages of breaking down the tradeshow and the week had been a huge success. She'd just gotten off the phone with Harrison and he informed her that he'd been hearing positive things so far. There'd been a few blips but overall, it had run smoothly.

Better than all that, that psycho Glenn White wasn't in Vegas. It made it easier to move around today without feeling as if a dark cloud was hanging over her. Quinn had been more relaxed too.

As she strode down one of the aisles of displays being broken down, her cell phone buzzed. "Yeah?" she answered, immediately recognizing the number of the owner of the catering company.

"Athena, it's Jodi. I've got a bit of a situation. There's a van that's not supposed to be parked by the kitchen exits and it's blocking one of our vans. I can't figure out who it belongs to but I need it moved because we're almost loaded up."

"Where are you now?"

"Kitchen."

"I'll be there in a sec." She ended the call then held up a hand to signal Raegan, who was talking to one of the vendors.

Smiling brightly, as seemed to be the norm for Raegan, she strode over, her heels clicking quickly with her movements. She wasn't that much taller than Athena, maybe five feet five or six, but she was a lean woman and it made her appear taller. Today she'd pulled her dark hair back into a twist at her nape. "Hey, boss."

Athena snorted. "Stop calling me that." She was only two years older and it felt weird.

"Only if you stop snorting when I do it." Raegan's grin just grew wider as she fell into step. "So what are we doing now?"

"Tiny emergency in the kitchen."

"Today's been pretty smooth though, or at least it seems like it, right?" she asked as they sidestepped a vendor breaking down a display of GPS systems.

"Exceptionally so."

"Can I ask you something totally non-work related?"

Athena shot her a glance. "Ah, sure."

"Have you ever dated more than one guy at once?"

She had to think about it. Quinn might be her first lover, but she'd dated in college. Well, a little, the last two years of it. Once she'd been more comfortable in her skin dating had been somewhat more enjoyable. "Not really. I mean, I went on dates in college, sometimes with a different guy week to week, but I was never exclusive with any of them and now that I think about it, I guess there wasn't any overlap." Because deep down, she was a one man kind of woman.

"Okay." Raegan's pretty mouth pulled into a frown as they reached the kitchen.

The volume level instantly raised as they stepped inside, the voices seeming to echo in the smaller space. "Uh uh, you can't leave me hanging like that. Why are you asking?"

Athena wasn't exactly surprised when Raegan's cheeks flushed. "I had a couple dinner dates with one of the security guys from the hotel this week. We've only kissed, but today, oh, you remember the man we met Tuesday?" When Athena nodded, Raegan continued. "Well, he called to let me know he'd be in Miami next week and wanted to know if I wanted to have dinner with him."

She nodded approvingly. "Nice." Rhys Maxwell was a handsome man by any standard. Blond hair, blue eyes, he looked more like a tan surfer than a billionaire with holdings in… well, whatever. Lots and lots of stuff.

"I don't know why I was getting hung up. I mean, I only went on a couple dates and it's not like we talked about the future—I *leave* tomorrow. I don't know why I feel so guilty saying yes." The frown was back.

She didn't respond because it sounded like Raegan was having an internal battle more than looking for real advice. Athena called out to one of the servers from the show. "Where's Jodi?"

Though he was in the middle of packing up serving trays, he nodded to one of the exit doors. "Out back."

"Thanks." As she and Raegan maneuvered their way through the expansive kitchen, she frowned when she realized the exit door was propped open and there was no security guard standing there. She'd been very specific with the entire staff about this, both in-house and outside hires. If any doors remained open there *had* to be a guard.

"That's not supposed to be open, is it?" Raegan asked, concern in her voice.

"No, it's not." And Jodi was going to get an earful when Athena found her.

Outside a chilly breeze rolled over them. A van with the catering company's logo was backed right up to the exit door but there was more than enough room to maneuver around it. The interior was half-packed but she didn't spot a driver or any other employees around.

When she stepped around to the side of the van she realized what Jodi had been talking about. This section of the hotel was for employees only and was more or less a loading area, with a row of ramps for vans or delivery trucks to come and go.

Another van with a florist logo on the side was parked directly in front of the caterer's. Sighing, she pulled out her cell and called Jodi.

When she heard a phone ringing, she continued down the side of the ramp, looking for Jodi. As Athena reached the front of the other van, an icy fist clenched around her chest. Raegan sucked in a breath behind her.

A man was crouched down in front of the vehicle, holding Jodi's phone—and a gun.

"Drop your phone," he said quietly. With a thick beard that had to be fake, a ball cap and sunglasses, Glenn White wasn't easily recognizable but she knew his voice immediately. It sent chills scratching down her spine.

Athena wanted to run, but there was nowhere to go. The drop off the ramp was too high up and if she tried to backtrack she'd just slam into Raegan.

"Both of you. Do it or I shoot. I'll start with your knees." His voice was dead calm as he lowered the weapon, aiming right for her knees. The calmness scared her more than anything. Like he'd have absolutely no problem just pumping her full of bullets.

Heart thudding, Athena did as he said, praying that someone from the kitchen saw them and alerted security. Or that someone in actual security saw them. There were plenty of surveillance cameras out here. Seconds ticked by, but felt like eons as she stared at the gun.

Next to her Raegan let her phone fall too. It clattered to the ramp.

Gun out, he pointed it at them menacingly. "Move to the back of the van."

With no choice but to do as he said, they both started backtracking along the side of the van. Athena couldn't stop the fear filtering through her or the thoughts of

Quinn. The thing developing between them was intense and amazing. The thought of losing it all because of a lunatic was too surreal.

"Stop," White ordered as they reached it.

Athena knew he was going to put them in there and she refused to go. He would kill her anyway. She'd rather die here than her family never knowing what happened to her. "You can fucking shoot me but I'm not getting in there." Her voice came out surprisingly strong. Inside, however, she was trembling with terror. He hadn't actually ordered them in the van but she knew it was coming.

"Fine, how about I shoot her?" White grabbed Raegan by the arm and held the gun to her temple.

Oh, God. Athena's stomach roiled. Raegan's eyes were huge, her skin pale and... her smart watch caught the light. A tiny glimmer of hope flickered through Athena, but her terror pushed most of it back. She couldn't let Glenn see it anyway. She held up her hands. "I'll get in but please leave her here. She's not part of this."

He just snorted and shoved Raegan at her before opening the back door to the van. Then he tossed them zip ties. "Tie your wrists together tight. Use your teeth to pull it closed. Make it quick." He glanced down the side of the other van, his agitation clear.

They did as he said, then climbed into the back of the empty van, urged on by his gun. There was nothing but two metal poles running along the ceiling. She'd seen dry-cleaning vans before that delivered and they'd had the same layout.

Smiling, he pulled out two sets of cuffs. "Glad I came prepared with two."

He jumped in the back with them and slammed the rear doors shut, using his gun as a barrier. As he started to hook Raegan's wrists to the pole, Athena rolled back from her kneeling position and kicked at his chest. It was hard with her odd position and secured wrists, but she clipped him in the thigh with her heel.

Grunting in what sounded more like annoyance than anything else, he moved lightning quick, slamming his fist into her jaw before she could defend herself. Pain shot through her face.

"Fucking bitch," she heard him mutter as her head lolled back. She didn't pass out, but everything around her was hazy.

"Oh my God! Athena, are you okay?" Raegan's voice sounded far away.

It hurt too much to answer, but she was aware of her wrists being raised, then heard the distinctive click of the handcuffs around the pole.

As if from the far end of a tunnel she heard him moving from the cargo area to the driver's seat. The van rumbled to life and she jerked backward, sliding against the cold metal floor until she thumped against the door.

"Athena, talk to me," Raegan whispered.

"I'm okay," she managed to push out. She was pretty certain he hadn't broken her jaw since she could talk.

She wanted to tell Raegan that Quinn and Travis would find them, that the smart watch Raegan had on might save them if the guys remembered she was wearing it. But she was afraid White would hear her so she kept her mouth shut and prayed.

CHAPTER TWELVE

Quinn was about to slip his cell phone back into his pocket when it rang in his hand. When he saw Iris's name he answered immediately. "Yeah?"

"We've got a problem with the video surveillance in the west sector… directly outside the kitchen the tradeshow staff are using." He was already moving before she'd finished. He'd seen Athena heading to the kitchen and Iris wouldn't be calling him unless this was important. Quinn grabbed Travis by the arm, but didn't say anything as he started moving through the vendors packing up their displays. He didn't need to. They'd worked together enough to operate as a unit.

Iris continued. "I've got guys on the way to check it out but previous feeds show a woman who owns the catering company heading outside, then Athena and Raegan not long after. Now we don't have a visual… It's coming back on. Something's not right." She cursed.

His heart stuttered in his chest. It was just a computer glitch, he told himself. "I'm on my way there now." Quinn and Travis moved through the kitchen, ignoring the shouts of protest as they barreled through two men carrying a stack of glasses.

"The fucking door is propped open," he growled, barely registering the sound of glass shattering behind him. They burst outside. He motioned to Travis to move around the right side of the catering van while he went around the left side.

"I see you guys," Iris said.

Withdrawing his weapon, he continued down the side of the van. If there was a threat Iris would have seen it on her end, but he wasn't taking a chance. Where the hell was Athena? If she'd come out here, there was nowhere else to go except out to one of the roads that ran through the hotel and casino's property.

As he rounded the front of the van, Travis did the same on the opposite side. Quinn's heart felt as if it stopped dead in his chest when he saw Athena and Raegan's phones on the ground. He recognized the cases to both. Fear surged up, raw and cold in his chest. "Call the cops now. They've been taken," he said to Iris, not needing to specify who. His gut told him who was behind the kidnapping too. "Check your exterior cams—"

"Wait," Travis said, snagging his own phone out of his pocket. His fingers moved across the screen at a rapid speed.

Quinn could hear Iris in the background shouting out orders, but he tuned her out as Travis spoke. "Remember the vendor that gave us all the smart watches?" He twisted his wrist once to show he was wearing his. Quinn didn't respond, but Travis didn't seem to expect him to. "Raegan and I have been going to the gym here every morning and using them. There's a GPS on them and I know she's got hers activated because we created free accounts. I've got full access to hers… there!" He held out his phone. A red dot was moving along a marked road on a virtual map. "She's moving at forty-five miles per hour right now."

Heart pounding an erratic thump against his chest, Quinn scooped up the phones on the ground. "You hear that Iris?" he asked as he jerked open the door to the catering van. He didn't have to tell Travis to shut the back doors, he was already doing it by the time Quinn slid into the front seat. Luckily he didn't have to hotwire the vehicle or waste time trying to hunt down someone with keys. They were sitting in the ignition.

"Yeah," she said as he started the engine. "I'm calling the police regardless. Stay on the line."

He set his phone down on the center console and started the ignition. Travis jumped in and Quinn jerked the van into drive. Years of training kept his movements calm and precise as Travis indicated which direction he should go. But inside, he felt as if his entire world was splitting apart at the seams.

Someone had taken Athena and Raegan and Quinn's gut told him it was White. He was supposed to be in Miami, far away from them. She was supposed to have been safe. Quinn was going with his gut though, this wasn't some random coincidence. White must have figured out a way to fool the Red Stone guys. It terrified Quinn that Athena was likely with him right now. The guy was a bastard who hadn't cared about hurting his own wife. Athena would just be a tool to him. Quinn could only hope White wanted to keep her alive to lure Quinn to him. Fuck it, Quinn should have been with her. He decided to berate himself later when she was safe and in his arms.

"Looks like they're slowing down, hmm, hold on." Travis rattled off an address.

"That's a rundown shopping strip," Iris said immediately, clearly recognizing the location. "Wyatt bought it recently. He's going to renovate it. There's a pawn shop, tattoo parlor, and ah, an old barber shop there I think. Couple other empty shops. Nothing's been open for about five months but even before that the places were pretty bad."

"She's stopped completely." Travis held out his phone for Quinn to see.

"Don't tell the cops where we're going," Quinn said as Travis used a map app on his phone to plug in the address where Raegan—*and please God, let Athena be with her*—was.

"Hell, Quinn." Iris sighed.

"If they show up sirens blazing we lose the element of surprise. Travis and I are both trained. We get in to where he's holding them, save them. If the cops show up you know as well as I do that it could turn into a hostage situation." If that happened, it was anyone's bet what would happen. Especially if White was the one who'd taken them. He'd been a cop and understood hostage negotiations and tactics. And he was also unpredictable as hell.

"All right. You want backup?"

"No."

She was silent for a long moment. "Too fucking bad. I'm on my way."

"We're not waiting."

"I know. Be careful, Devil Dog."

If he hadn't been so terrified for Athena he might have smiled. "Ooh Rah." He disconnected and glanced at Travis. "I don't want to wait for backup. You're free to wait though." Quinn knew Travis wouldn't but wanted to put the offer out there. He was going in no matter what. According to the map they'd be there in less than five minutes considering all the traffic laws he was breaking.

Travis just snorted in derision. "From the grid of Raegan's GPS map, I can't be sure, but it looks like the driver parked behind the shopping strip. And it appears as if she entered through the pawn shop rear door."

"Do a search, see if there's somewhere nearby we can park and enter through the back." Because if this was White, he was likely working alone. While he might want to, the bastard couldn't cover every exit. He sure as hell hadn't realized Raegan had on a smart watch. Maybe he didn't even know what the thing was.

Unfortunately he wouldn't have to cover every angle, all it would take was one bullet from White to take away the woman who'd come to mean everything to Quinn.

Glancing briefly in the side mirror he swerved into the next lane of traffic, cutting someone off. He ignored the blast of the horn as he took a sharp turn. He had to get to Athena.

Hang on, sweetheart.

* * *

"This guy is out of his mind," Raegan whispered.

Athena nodded, her throat tight with fear. White had brought them to an abandoned shop of some kind and shoved them in a matchbox-sized windowless office. She could hear him outside it, pacing, and knew he'd hear them if they attempted an escape. There was nowhere to go anyway unless they wanted to 1) attempt kicking through a wall or 2) climb through the ceiling tiles. He would hear them if they tried to do either of those things and there was nothing in the tiny room they could use as a weapon either.

She desperately wanted to say something to Raegan about the smart watch, but didn't want to draw any attention to it. Athena was terrified that the guys hadn't thought of it. They'd all been given one, but still. She'd remembered but Quinn and Travis might not.

Suddenly the door swung open. White had ditched the ball cap and sunglasses. She had no problem recognizing him now even with the beard. He flicked a glance at Athena, but focused on Raegan, something almost apologetic in his dark eyes.

"You weren't supposed to be with her," he said, just a hint of regret in his voice.

Athena realized he intended to kill Raegan when he took a menacing step forward. She popped up from the rickety chair she'd been sitting on and blurted, "You want to know where your wife is. Suzanne, right?"

His gaze snapped to hers, laser sharp and bright with a kind of wild madness that made her shudder. "What do you know about Suzanne?" His breathing increased, the madness intensifying.

Cold sweat trickled down Athena's spine. "I just know that she left, disappeared. And Quinn knows where she is." A total lie but she needed to keep this madman talking. "If you kill Raegan or me you'll never find out where she is. We're you're only bargaining chips. You *need* us alive if you ever want to see your wife again." Athena was rambling now but desperately wanted to stall him.

"I only need one of you to negotiate," he snapped.

She swallowed hard. "If you kill her now you lose a bargaining chip. And..." Athena decided to play the only card she had. The only thing she could really think of since the mention of White's ex-wife wasn't working as well as she'd hoped. "Raegan is Keith Caldwell's niece. His *only* niece." That part wasn't true but whatever.

White's hand shook, his gaze jerking over to Raegan.

Athena needed his focus on her though. "You know who he is then. And you know what will happen if you kill her. He and his sons will hunt you to the ends of the earth. I'm just a Red Stone employee, a new one at that. Killing Raegan guarantees you die."

"Fuck, fuck, *fuck.*" He glanced away from them for a moment and she could practically see the wheels of the crazy-train in his head turning.

At a soft thudding sound from somewhere nearby, Athena's heart jumped in her throat. She prayed it was Quinn. Or the police. *Someone.*

White stiffened and immediately reached for her. He yanked her upper arm and tugged her to him. She cried out in pain until he shoved the gun right to her temple. "Shut the fuck up."

Swallowing hard, she nodded once, afraid to move more than that. Her entire body was numb as he nudged her forward. The only pain she was really aware of was her throbbing jaw from when he'd punched her. But she could deal with a little pain.

"Stay in front of me and don't try anything stupid." His breath was hot against her ear, making bile rise in her throat.

She could smell alcohol too, beer maybe. He moved the gun away from her head and for a moment she allowed a shred of relief to slide through her—until he pressed it against her ribs.

He pushed her forward, but never lost his grip on her upper arm as they moved through a doorway. There was no door, just a frame.

Slivers of light filtered through windows that had been boarded up. There were a couple dozen display cases but they all appeared empty. There was a musty scent in here that hadn't been in the back. Flickers of dust floated through the beams of light, as if something had just been disturbed.

"Show yourself or I blow her fucking head off." White's voice was quiet, deadly.

She didn't see anyone else and she couldn't hear anything, but maybe he'd seen something. Or maybe he was just guessing Quinn had come after her. Oh God, what if there was no one here and he shot her because—

Travis rose quietly from behind one of the cases, his expression practically feral. She'd never seen him look like that, like... a killer. His weapon was pointed at them but it made her feel better. At least if White shot her, Travis would take him out. Quinn had to be here somewhere too. Fear for both Quinn and Travis surged through her, battling with hope that they were here to save her and Raegan.

"Step out from behind that case and drop your weapon. Now!" White barked.

Travis moved slowly from behind the display case. As he did, White moved too, using Athena as a shield. Travis hadn't dropped his weapon though. Athena could barely move, was so numb with terror. Everything was surreal, as if she was watching all this happen to someone else.

"Drop it!" White pointed his gun at Travis, his hand steady.

In that moment Travis dove to the side. She had a millisecond to question it. Something wet sprayed over the back of her neck as White's gun fired.

The blast made her jump. She screamed as one of the boarded up front windows exploded, glass and wood splintering. Before she could register what had happen, White wasn't gripping her anymore. His gun fell to the floor.

She started to turn when two strong hands gripped her arms tight from behind and swiveled her around. It took a moment for everything to fall into place.

"You're okay, sweetheart," Quinn said, his voice unsteady. Worry bled into his eyes as he ran his hands up and down her arms, looking for wounds. He cut her zip-tie free in a second.

She felt weird, numb as she looked down at White. He was dead, his throat slit, blood pouring onto the floor. Quinn must have done it while Travis distracted him. She shivered, thinking that anything could have gone wrong. But it hadn't.

"Tell me you're okay!" Quinn shook her a little.

The command in his voice snapped her out of her thoughts. Focusing on him, she saw a huge, skilled man with raw fear in his dark eyes. The sight clawed at her. "I'm fine. Are you... hurt?" Another dose of panic punched through her. Now she started to scan him, but he just tugged her into his arms in a bear hug. The feel of him holding her close was too much to handle. She finally felt safe.

She wrapped her arms around him, burying her face against his neck and let the tears come. "You guys found us," she sobbed out, unable to stop the tears.

"You're wearing a smart watch from now on too," he murmured, his voice right next to her ear.

She wanted to get away from White's body and out of this disgusting place but more than anything, she just wanted to hold on to Quinn. She needed to reassure herself that he was really here and she was safe.

"I fucking love you," Quinn murmured against her ear. "I don't care if it's too soon to say it. I love you."

She pulled back and grabbed his face between her hands. "You're not telling me that with a dead body a few feet away!"

To her surprise he let out a loud, harsh laugh and scooped her up in his arms. "Let's get the hell out of here then and let the cops deal with this garbage." Undeniable rage threaded the last couple words as he strode through the building toward the back.

When he stepped through the back door with her in his arms, she sucked in a breath of fresh air and wanted to start crying all over again. Out of the corner of her eye she saw Travis and Raegan by one of the vans but all her focus was on Quinn. "You can put me down now."

He resisted for a moment but did as she said. She cupped his cheeks, gentler this time, as her heels touched the ground. "I love you too."

EPILOGUE

Four months later

"What are you grumbling about under your breath?" Quinn pressed the elevator button and glanced at Athena, humor in his voice.

"Nothing, I'm just annoyed. Like this couldn't wait until Monday?" Harrison had asked her to check the rooftop dining area of a new, exclusive hotel that would be opening in about a month. She'd been planning to check it out anyway, but he'd asked her ten minutes before she was supposed to leave for work. And he'd been insistent she see it tonight—even though he knew she had birthday plans.

"It's okay if we miss the reservation. This is your work." Quinn wrapped an arm around her and tugged her close as they stepped inside.

She wanted to press her nose against his neck and inhale. The man had a spicy, masculine scent that drove her crazy. Ever since that insanity in Vegas they'd been pretty much inseparable during their off-work hours. She couldn't get enough of him. It still scared her what could have happened to them. To all of them. She and Raegan had enrolled in self-defense classes since returning to Miami and it gave Athena a sense of control. Thankfully Quinn had been cleared quickly in White's death and the caterer White had knocked out had been found unconscious but alive. Unfortunately he'd killed someone else who worked for the catering company. White had been careful and smart jamming the security feed at the casino. Not to mention using his cousin to make it appear as if he was still in Miami. Athena wondered if he'd have gotten away with kidnapping her and Raegan—in addition to his other crimes and planned crimes—if it hadn't been for Raegan's smart watch and Quinn and Travis's training. Fighting off a shudder, she shelved that thought. She couldn't worry about 'what-if's' anymore.

"I know, but I realize how hard it was to get that reservation. I don't want to be late." She squeezed him back. Her birthday was tomorrow and Quinn had gone to a lot of trouble to get a reservation for them at one of her favorite places. He seemed more excited than her about her birthday. She knew it was a little nerdy, but she'd never celebrated a birthday with a boyfriend before and she wanted to enjoy this one.

He kissed the top of her head as the elevator came to a soft halt and dinged. A sensual, husky female voice announced that they had 'reached their destination and to have a pleasant day'.

She snickered as they stepped out into the tiled space of the dim dining area. "What do you want to bet it was a man's idea to have that audio program installed?"

Before Quinn could respond, lights snapped on and too many people to count shouted "Surprise!"

She nearly jumped out of her skin. A happy birthday sign had been hung above a bar and her parents and too many friends to count all stood there wearing silly birthday hats and grins on their faces. She couldn't find her voice and fought the tears that pricked her eyes. She squeezed Quinn's side. "You did this?" she asked, looking up at him.

"Happy birthday," Quinn murmured, kissing the top of her head.

She pulled him into a tight hug, unable to find her voice. Her throat clogged with tears at the sweet gesture.

Nearly two hours later, after a few too many glasses of champagne, cake, and mingling with her family and friends, she found herself blessedly alone with Quinn on one of the open balconies.

"You're very sneaky." She let him take her glass, watched in pleasure as he set it on one of the high top tables. She just loved to watch him move. He had a gracefulness that seemed incongruous with his size.

When he turned back to her and sank down on one knee, it took a moment for her champagne-addled brain to realize what he was doing. His hands shook, something that surprised her, as he pulled out a small box and popped it open. "Marry me?"

She stared at his face, not even glancing at the ring, then threw herself into his arms. "Yes!" Since he was still crouching she nearly toppled him over.

Laughing, he slid the ring on her finger and stood, gathering her into his arms.

"You're going to have a hard time topping this birthday next year—or ever." Talk about the best gift. She'd known they were heading in this direction but hadn't expected it anytime soon.

"I love you, Athena." His eyes glinted in that wicked way as he crushed his mouth over hers.

As their tongues danced together, she briefly wondered if they could find a private place to sneak off to before the night ended. The balcony was private from prying ears but anyone could see them from inside. And she wasn't an exhibitionist by any stretch.

When he pulled her even tighter, she melted into him, thankful to have found such an incredible man. She'd never expected to fall in love so hard or so fiercely, but now that she had, she was never letting him go.

Thank you for reading Sworn to Protect. I really hope you enjoyed it and that you'll consider leaving a review at one of your favorite online retailers.

If you would like to read more, turn the page for a sneak peek of more of my work. And if you don't want to miss any future releases, please feel free to join my newsletter. I only send out a newsletter for new releases or sales news. Find the signup link on my website: http://www.katiereus.com

SHATTERED DUTY
Deadly Ops Series
Copyright © 2015 Katie Reus

That grip tightened again but this time he started rubbing his first two fingers against her neck in a soft little rhythm. The action was almost erotic. Or maybe that was just the effect he was having on her. She could feel his gentle stroking all the way to the pulsing point between her legs. Maybe she had mental issues that this man was turning her on.

He leaned closer, skimming his mouth against her jawline and she froze. Just completely, utterly froze. "Are you meeting Tasev?" he whispered.

She'd told herself to be prepared for this question, to keep her reaction under wraps, but he came to his own conclusion if his savage curse was anything to go by. Damn it, Wesley was going to be pissed at her, but Levi had been right. She had operational latitude right now and she needed to keep Levi close. They needed to know what he knew and what he was planning. Trying to shut him out now, when he was at the party specifically to meet the German, would be stupid. Levi had stayed off their radar for two years because he was good. Of course Wesley hadn't exactly sent out a worldwide manhunt for him either. About a year ago he'd decided to more or less let him go.

Now . . . "I met with the German earlier tonight. He squeezed me in before some of his other meetings."

Levi snorted, his gaze dipping to her lips once more, that hungry look in place again. It was so raw and in her face it was hard to ignore that kind of desire and what it was doing to her. "I can understand why."

Even though Levi didn't ask she decided to use the latitude she had and bring him in on this. They had similar goals. She needed to bring Tasev down and rescue a very important scientist—if he was even the man who'd sent out an emergency message to Meghan/Wesley—but that didn't mean she couldn't let Levi have Tasev once she'd gotten what she needed. "I'm meeting with Tasev tomorrow night."

At her words every muscle in Levi's lean, fit body stilled.

Before he could respond, she continued, "I'll make you a deal. You can come with me to the meeting—if we can work out an agreeable plan—but you don't kill him until I get what I want. I have less than a week. Can you live with that time line?" She was allowed to bring one person with her to the meeting so it would be Levi—if he could be a professional and if Wesley went for it. And of course, if Tasev did. They had a lot to discuss before she was on board one hundred percent, but bringing along a seasoned agent—former agent—like Levi could be beneficial.

Levi watched her carefully again, his gaze roaming over her face, as if he was trying to see into her mind. "You're not lying. Why are you doing this?"

"Because if I try to shut you out you'll cause me

more problems than I want to deal with. And I don't want to kill you."

Those dark eyes narrowed a fraction with just a hint of amusement—as if he knew she couldn't take him on physically. "And?"

"And . . . I owe you." Selene didn't explain because she knew he'd think she was referring to when Meghan saved her life. That was fine with her. Telling him exactly how she owed him would strip her open too bare and she wasn't willing to let anyone see that vulnerable side of her.

"Telling the truth again." He frowned now, true confusion in his gaze. Whether from her words or the fact that she was letting him in on this op. "You plan to try to bring me in after the op?"

"No." That was actually the truth. Wesley, however, was a different story. But she refused to let her mind go there, knowing Levi would pick up on it.

Levi started to respond when a burst of gunfire from the pool area made them both turn at the noise. Selene automatically moved off the bench, crouching down behind it and to her surprise Levi moved in front of her, blocking her even though they were too far away to be in any danger from what she could hear.

"This is what happens when you get a bunch of criminals under the same roof," he muttered.

She snorted in agreement. "I'm leaving using the beach. You're free to join me." There hadn't been any more gunfire so likely the guards had the situation under control but she wasn't heading back up there. She'd already had her meeting so she had no reason to return.

Now he snorted as he turned to face her, still crouching low. He slid his long, callused hands down her bare arms. This time she couldn't hide the shiver. "Oh, I'm joining you," he murmured, a seductive note in his voice.

But the timing was all wrong. For once she wished she understood the opposite sex more. What was he doing? She'd already told him he could come on the op with her. Her nipples tightened and her body hummed with a strange anticipation as he lightly held her wrists in both hands, his thumbs rubbing her inner wrist in small circles. She started to pull back and he let go of one of her wrists. As she pushed out a sigh of relief, the feel of cold steel skimmed her skin just as the soft snick of handcuffs clicked into place.

ACKNOWLEDGMENTS

Writing a story is just the first step in producing the final book and I'm grateful for the people who help with all the other steps in between. Kari Walker, eleven books into this series, and I'm incredibly thankful for your continuous words of wisdom. Thank you to Joan Turner for your attention to detail. Jaycee of Sweet 'N Spicy Designs thank you for your beautiful design work. Sarah Romsa, thank you for keeping me sane and taking care of all the behind-the-scenes stuff. As always, I'm grateful for my supportive husband and son. Last but not least, I'm also thankful to God.

COMPLETE BOOKLIST

Red Stone Security Series
No One to Trust
Danger Next Door
Fatal Deception
Miami, Mistletoe & Murder
His to Protect
Breaking Her Rules
Protecting His Witness
Sinful Seduction
Under His Protection
Deadly Fallout
Sworn to Protect

The Serafina: Sin City Series
First Surrender
Sensual Surrender
Sweetest Surrender
Dangerous Surrender

Deadly Ops Series
Targeted
Bound to Danger
Chasing Danger (novella)

Shattered Duty
Edge of Danger

Non-series Romantic Suspense
Running From the Past
Everything to Lose
Dangerous Deception
Dangerous Secrets
Killer Secrets
Deadly Obsession
Danger in Paradise
His Secret Past
Retribution

Paranormal Romance
Destined Mate
Protector's Mate
A Jaguar's Kiss
Tempting the Jaguar
Enemy Mine
Heart of the Jaguar

Moon Shifter Series
Alpha Instinct
Lover's Instinct (novella)
Primal Possession
Mating Instinct
His Untamed Desire (novella)
Avenger's Heat

Hunter Reborn
Protective Instinct (novella)

Darkness Series
Darkness Awakened
Taste of Darkness
Beyond the Darkness

ABOUT THE AUTHOR

Katie Reus is the *New York Times* and *USA Today* bestselling author of the Red Stone Security series, the Moon Shifter series and the Deadly Ops series. She fell in love with romance at a young age thanks to books she pilfered from her mom's stash. Years later she loves reading romance almost as much as she loves writing it.

However, she didn't always know she wanted to be a writer. After changing majors many times, she finally graduated summa cum laude with a degree in psychology. Not long after that she discovered a new love. Writing. She now spends her days writing dark paranormal romance and sexy romantic suspense.

For more information on Katie please visit her website: www.katiereus.com. Also find her on twitter @katiereus or visit her on facebook at:
www.facebook.com/katiereusauthor.

Made in the USA
San Bernardino, CA
19 May 2018